Opioid, Indiana

Also by the author

Sip

Opioid, Indiana

....

Brian Allen Carr

Illustrations by Jim Agpalza

Published by
Soho Press Inc.
853 Broadway
New York, NY 10003

Library of Congress Cataloging-in-Publication Data

Carr, Brian Allen, 1979– author.
Opioid, Indiana / Brian Allen Carr.

ISBN 978-1-64129-078-4
eISBN 978-1-64129-079-1

I. Title

PS3603.A772 O66 2019 813'.6—dc23 2019004391

Interior art by Jim Agpalza
Interior design by Janine Agro, Soho Press, Inc.

Printed in the United States of America

10 9 8 7 6 5 4 3 2 1

Opioid, Indiana

I'm from Texas, but most of this story takes place in Indiana, where the winter weather sits like iced gray vomit on the cornfields. Every restaurant serves fried pork sandwiches. Half the men over thirty-five are so numb on opioids you could win a bar fight just by swinging a dead cat over your head and running in circles. Not that I can get into a bar. Shit, I'm seventeen.

In Indiana kids my age vape with nothing in it but flavor. Might as well eat candy fog. I'm not the biggest fan of getting fucked up, but if I'm doing something, I'm doing it for real. None of the Mexicans I knew in Texas vaped and I never chilled with whites before moving to Indiana. They're fine. I'm one of them. But I'm not gross. I don't sit around eating food-stamp Frosted Flakes while ragging on black folks because they're looking for handouts. I don't scream "Build the Wall" every time I hear a language other than English.

Whites aren't supposed to talk race, and I didn't realize that until I came here. Back home, almost everyone's Mexican American or Mexican Mexican, so we'd talk about being white all the time, because my non-white friends were curious, and mostly back home when you talked about being white, you'd talk about how mean white people's parents are. Mexican kids never get told to leave home. They can live in converted garages until they're seventy-five years old and not a single soul would judge them.

If you're nineteen and white and not paying a grand a month for an apartment, you're a piece of shit. Whites can't keep long in their parents' nests. Gobbling up their parents' food. Watching cartoons on their parents' cable.

White folks also get bad sunburns, and that was the other thing my friends would ask about. I'd show up with pink cheeks on some Monday and they'd ask if I was wearing makeup.

Maybe I didn't belong in South Texas. It's a place mean with heat, but Mexicans seemed at home there, standing on that thorny land with their backs to the sun. Singing hymns to Quetzalcoatl in nearly lost native languages. Hoping for rain. Healing off medicine made from plants. Rubbing eggs over babies' bellies to cure them of fever.

Indiana is mean with cold, but whites go wrong here too. They get too doughy. They get that Mountain Dew mouth. Like they brush their teeth with candy. Like the only time their hearts race is when they're screaming at news channels. Popping pills to catch boners. Popping other pills to get their dicks back to soft. And when I saw these white boys in Indiana vaping nothing but flavor, it about made me sick. Might as well boil some water, huff the steam and then chew gum. Jesus, take control of your dick and be somebody.

All that said—Texas is the greatest country on the planet and Indiana is the greatest state in the nation. Honestly, in some ways these Hoosiers are just Mexicans with white skin. They love cars and America and guns and the military, and that's just like Mexicans. And both old whites and old Mexicans are racists too.

Here's a story: I had an across-the-street neighbor back in McAllen, Texas, who used to mow lawns. He was ninety-four years old. I swear to God. He'd been in the military and he was as skinny as a suit on a coat hanger, and one day he came to my house and knocked on my door. I can't remember his name but it might've been Emilio. We talked all the time, but I only called him "Sir."

He was at my door and it was like this: "Hey, Riggle."

That's my name, and I was like, "Hey, Sir."

"Look," he told me. He unbuttoned his shirt and

widened his eyes. They were like gray fried eggs. A few different lifetimes swam in the color of them.

"What's that?"

He had a bandage on his chest that he pulled back and it sort of flapped open like a hanging white tongue to reveal a stapled-shut stretch of Sir's newly shaved chest. "Open heart surgery," he said.

"What the hell?"

"Touch it," he told me. It was like a dare. Like if I didn't I could never be a man, and he gazed away into some distant and masculine abyss. I laid my hand on the bumpy scar. "Quadruple bypass," he said, and my hand seemed to absorb some of the energy from his healing. "Do you have any beer?" He licked his lips and buttoned his shirt back. "The wife won't let me buy any, ever, since the operation."

My hand was still sort of tingling as I processed the request. "Should you be drinking?"

His mouth tightened. "Are you a doctor?"

I sniffed my hand. "Nah."

"Then do you have any beer?"

I always had beer. My guardian would buy cases of Lone Star and I'd pinch a few whenever, and hide them at the back of the vegetable drawer because my guardian was a fat ass. "Meet me out back."

I lived backed up to an alley, and we stood out there on

the asphalt in the heat of September sipping beers and he told me his tales as we both sweated in the sun.

"When I was about your age," he said, "I joined the army. I was stationed in *El Paso*." When he said the words *El Paso*, it was like the ghost of every Mexican Christmas Past came dancing a hat dance from out his throat. A tumbleweed drifted across a desert highway. Somewhere, a whip cracked. "There was a movie theater there," Sir said. "Me and all the boys would go." He took a long swig of his beer. Swallowed. Looked down the alley. "We were Mexican. Had to sit in the balcony. Can you imagine? Had to sit up there in our US Army uniforms just because our skin was brown."

There was terrific silence in the heat of the alley. You could smell the asphalt roads turning back into tar.

"That's terrible, Sir, I'm sorry."

"You think we'll ever have a Mexican president?" he asked. "In my lifetime?"

"Dunno. I hope so. Maybe. Women ones too." This was back when Obama was still president, before we knew Trump would be next.

"Hm," he said. "Just makes me mad we had a monkey before a Mexican." He drained his beer in one final and dramatic chug, and he chucked the empty can at the asphalt and it tipped and tapped down the way a bit until it came to a rest, glinting in the September sun. "Thanks for the drink," he told me. He pounded his chest with a fist. "I gotta mow some lawns."

He walked off and I drank the rest of my beer and kicked at weeds that grew through the cracked-open asphalt and thought to myself: Did Sir really call Obama a monkey? And in the context of that story? Like, in that theater in El Paso, where would Sir have had Obama sit?

Here is something that should shock you: in Indiana, there are Confederate flags everywhere. I mean, that's an exaggeration, but there are more than in Texas. And that is not an exaggeration. These corn growers fly the bars and stars all over. Two blocks away, this old dude's got a truck that has HERITAGE NOT HATRED painted on his tailgate above a rendition of Old Dixie, and that shit just eats me up. Whose heritage, struggler?

When I was growing up in Texas, I was always under the impression that the Confederate flag was something white Texans should be ashamed of. I mean, rednecks flew them, but rednecks would sneak into goat fields on moonlit nights to sex the doe goats. Call that losing your hick virginity. I always wondered what that smelled like. Out there in pasture. Your Wranglers tucked into your Red Wings. Thrusting back and forth as the messy she-thing bleated in the dew-wet grass.

These Hoosiers fly them bars and stars like they're paying homage to their forefathers. Their forefathers were heroes. My forefathers were Twilight Zoners. They wanted black men to pick their cotton and black women to swallow their seed, and they wanted to repay that work and humiliation with more work and humiliation. Why would you take up a thing I'm ashamed of from my past and claim it as your own?

I think it's a trick. It's like someone said, "So long as you fly this flag, the worst thing you'll ever be is a share-cropper." But I don't buy it. You can't get less slave. You can get less rich and you can get less poor, but you are a slave or you are not.

Right now I'm staying at my uncle's place. My last guardian, my dead father's cousin, got tired of me stealing his beer, and that's why I'm in Indiana, and that's why I've seen snow. Hell, some's falling right now. It drops like goose feathers and lands like white scabs on the skin of the world. The first few times I saw it, I got excited. Now it makes me depressed. The days have been gray for months. Schools across the country keep getting shot up by angry boys who can't get their dicks wet, and the president's always tweeting nonsense, and my uncle's girlfriend, Peggy, drives me crazy. In the sex way.

My uncle's been gone a few weeks, and Peggy is in the living room singing along to Brandi Carlile. I'm seventeen. I'm from Texas. I'm a struggler. Peggy is like, "Wherever is your heart I call home," and I'm like—my heart is in my chest and I'm in the next room yearning and last she talked to my uncle, he was off to binge-snort meth or drop low on Oxy. Off to hunch somewhere and wait for the firemen to hit him with Naloxone or maybe go out to chop down trees to cure his meth boredom. Meth heads will do it. Meth heads will do all kinds of weird meth shit. Hell, if we could just get honest, America could be the cleanest place on earth. You could have hordes of roving tweakers turning in sacks of litter they found on the highways for lines of meth. You could drop them in the ocean with snorkels to pick plastic off sea turtles' snouts. Surfacing every so often to smile their rotten teeth and hand over garbage and get more crank.

Peggy's the type of woman who falls in love for pain. Women do it. I know that around the country right now women are trying to change things, and I get it. Hell, a time or two I should've kicked my uncle's ass just on account of how he treated Peggy. But those times he was on meth. If he'd have been on painkillers, I might have thrown hands at him. But you can't fight someone who's on meth. They don't feel a thing. If you're on painkillers you can get your ass kicked. If you're on meth you're invincible.

But women like Peggy aren't always like the women

on the internet. I've got 174 Twitter followers, which isn't much but I don't have unlimited data, and I read my feed and I see what the people I follow post. But girls still date boys who are mean to them. Maybe not the honors girls or athletes or cheerleaders. The regular girls. The ones who are just there. And I guess all of that is fine. Do what you want. But don't be surprised when illogical shit leads to illogical shit.

Peggy will say she wants to be treated good, but she gave her heart away to a druggie.

I don't want to tell you the name of the town I'm in, so we'll call it Opioid, Indiana, and it's near Indianapolis, and I suppose it's home to me.

In Opioid, Indiana, there's this guy who rides a bicycle. He's got a sunken faraway look and he always pedals slow. He needs a haircut. His clothes are dirty. There's a Confederate flag stuck to the frame of his bike. It stands high above him and flaps in the breeze. He sets his wrists on his handlebars. Sometimes he's eating a sucker. He rolls the thing in his mouth. The white stick of it goes from the left corner of his mouth to the right corner of his mouth. He just pedals. Pedals. Pedals. He moves the sucker in his mouth again. It'll be 40 degrees and he'll be wearing a tank top. Colder than that, and he'll have on a sweater.

Through the streets, he cruises. Slow the way honey is slow when you're waiting for what's at the bottom of the bottle. He's so well-known in town, you could be him for Halloween.

There's this other guy called Autistic Ross. He's like the president of small talk. He wanders the streets and waves at children. He sits on this one corner and stares off at nothing. If he goes into anywhere, everyone hollers his name. He has funny teeth and he laughs like a child. If a few days go by and no one sees him, all the neighbors get worried. They stand on their porches and look up and down the street with their arms folded. When he shows back up, they all go inside.

Once at my high school, they passed around a sheet and the sheet asked what we wanted to be when we grew up, and I put either Autistic Ross or the Bicycling Confederate, and I got called into the counselor's office a few days after the Florida shooting, and I sat on a plastic chair in a room that smelled like dead flowers and listened to some piano music that tinkled in from some hidden speaker.

"We just wanted to talk," the counselor said after this awkward moment. "You put interesting things on this questionnaire. We asked you who your biggest influences were and you put 'dead people,' and we asked what you wanted to be when you grew up and you said Autistic Ross . . ."

"You know him?"

"Or the Bicycling Confederate . . ."

"These are people right? I mean, I'm not the only one who sees them."

"Oh, they're real." The counselor jostled papers. "But you can't be one of those. Not for a job. How will you live? It doesn't make sense."

"How do they live?"

The counselor's chin moved toward her shoulder and her eyes aimed at the sky. She inhaled. Her mouth went funny. "I don't know. But it's not just that. I mean, that symbol is hurtful. That flag he flies. And we know you're from the South."

"I'm not flying that flag. Do you see me with that flag?"

My counselor smiled. "No," she said. "But these are strange times."

"Agreed."

The counselor picked up my sheet, the one I'd filled out, then she set it on her desk and opened a drawer. She reached in and pulled out a vape pen. She looked down at it. "Do you know what this is?"

"A vape pen."

"Do you know where it's from?"

"I mean, you just took it out of your desk."

"Before that."

"Before that it was in your desk."

She got huffy. "A girl in one of your classes says it's yours. Says that she saw it fall from your bag."

"Okay."

"So it's yours?"

"If she says so. Who am I to question a female? It's my candy fog tube."

"Candy fog?"

"Vape," I said. "Flavored clouds."

She picked up her phone and dialed an extension. "This is a THC pen," she told me. "There is THC in this."

Holy fuck, I thought. I've been underestimating these Hoosiers. I thinned my eyes. "Oh, that ain't mine." I didn't realize what I had been volunteering to. "Looks like it though. Different though. Mine's at home. I just remembered." I didn't really have a vape pen, but the only way to stop a bad lie is with a good lie.

"Yes," she said into the receiver. "Yes, send security down for Riggle. Yes. Yes, he confessed."

"I mean only kinda," I said. "I mean, I might be a bit wrong." What was to become of me?

In the principal's office, they told me I'd be suspended the next Monday through Friday. I thought: *How the fuck is that supposed to teach me a lesson? I'm getting a vacation. A vape-cation.*

What follows is the story of that week.

Monday

Back when Mom was alive she told me how the days of the week got their name. We'd lay in bed and she'd make a shadow puppet on the wall with a flashlight, and she called the shadow puppet Remote and Remote knew about everything and he looked like this:

Mom said that his stories were *our* stories. And Mom would make his voice. A kind of whisper with an accent like Spanish or Russian, but neither of those exactly, and she would open and close his mouth as she spoke for him—his shadow moving along on the wall. In most of his stories, Remote was the hero. Here is how he told me Monday got its name:

Long ago, before time and shadows, when Remote was a very young Remote, there was a man named Mun who lived on the moon, and Mun could have no babies. There were no ladies up there for him to be making babies with.

Mun was very sad. He wanted to be a father, because he had an infinite beard that was long and glowed, and he wanted a child to sit on his lap and pull the beard and giggle.

Desperate, Mun would stand on the edge of the moon and call down to Earth. He would say, "Down there! People of Earth! Send me a son." He would tie a basket to the end of his infinite beard and lower the basket to the Earth's surface but no reply would come. "I'd also settle for a daughter," Mun yelled. But every time he hauled up his basket, it would be empty.

He would wander across the sunlit moon. There was no weather. His footprints never faded. You could trace his whole life, follow his tracks to the dark side of the moon, and see where he had curled up in his beard to cry and be lonely.

On Earth, there was a great murderer. His name was Kal the Ender. He was called the Ender because he'd taken so many lives. He would kill fathers in front of their sons and then kill those sons in front of their mothers, and then he would poke out the sons' mothers' eyes so the last thing they saw before being blinded was the death of their loved ones, and he kept them in a cage near his bed so that the music of their lamentations became the lullabies for him to snooze to.

Kal the Ender was super twisted.

The people of Earth grew wary of him, but they didn't know what to do.

Wherever they imprisoned Kal the Ender, he would escape.

Then I, Remote, devised a plan. "On the moon," I said to the Earthlings, "there is one called Mun who desperately wants a son, and we might implore him to take Kal the Ender off our hands to raise as his own."

It was one of the best ideas they had ever had, because this was long before Earthlings thought of cool things. This was way before medicine and way before automobiles.

Remote climbed the tallest mountain and I shouted up at Mun my proposition. To take Kal the Ender off our hands.

"I hadn't really hoped to have a murderer son," Mun said.

"He won't have murdered anyone on the moon," I said. "And, most of his problems stem from bad parenting. You will be a great father, and Kal the Ender will change his ways."

Mun liked the sound of that. "I'll take him," he said.

Of course, Kal the Ender would not go on his own, so Remote invented a trap. We put several dozen boys at the end of a path, and just in front of the boys, we put a snare made from Mun's infinite beard.

Kal the Ender was told of the boys, and he hurried off down the path to catch them and murder them.

Alas, when he got just about where they were, Mun gave a great tug on his beard and hoisted Kal into the heavens.

Once Kal was gone, a great order came to the lives of the Earthlings. This was in large part due to the fact that Mun was not as good of a parent as he thought he would be.

Once every so often, Kal would kill Mun. But every time he died, Mun's infinite beard revived him. You could tell when Mun was dead, because you couldn't see the moon. The moon's cycle—when it was there and when it was gone—we called months. The months were divided into weeks. The weeks into days. And Remote charted the days on the Graph of Kal the Ender. The first of those days, Remote called Monday after Mun on the moon. How the months were named and how weeks came to be is a story no one remembers.

The only thing that makes my best friend, Bennet, half-black is his hair. Well, that and his daddy. But if you shaved his head with a razor he could pass as white. I mean, he'd look sick or something, but you'd think he was a struggler. Back during Jim Crow, that's what he would've done, but these days it's best to be black, so he lets it get fluffy. Don't get me wrong, I'm sure when he sees a cop he wishes his hair was gone, and every time we go into a convenience store, the clerks are always trying to decide whether or not they should follow him to see if he steals, but on the internet he's got it made. He's got like eight hundred Twitter followers and he can only get online on my phone. His mom hates the internet.

When Bennet heard I was suspended, he told his mom he was too scared to go to school on Monday on account of the shootings, so she let him stay home, but she made him promise to go back the next day.

"I'm not raising sissies," she told him.

"She gonna let you out the house, or she gonna make you stay inside?" I asked when Bennet told me.

"How's she gonna know? And we should've had Presidents' Day off anyhow."

"Yeah, I bet you wanted to celebrate Trump. Make him a card or something. Send it up to the White House."

"Shit. I ain't one of the 'good ones.'"

I had decided to be productive with my week off. I was gonna follow the Bicycling Confederate just to see what his game was, but I felt like that would be a weird thing to ask Bennet to do, and I didn't want to tell Bennet we couldn't hang on account of that. Can you imagine? He asks to hang out and I'm like, "Nah, bruh, I'm gonna follow that Bicycling Confederate."

So, I decided to sleep in on Monday and hang that day with Bennet, but I forgot to tell Peggy and she came pounding on my door at six-fifteen. "Get up, get up." She yelped, and moved instead to pound her palm on the wall close to my bed.

I had stayed up late the night before watching YouTube videos. One was like a breakdown of Kendrick Lamar's lyric "What's the yams" from the track "King Kunta." It showed all the literary references from his bars. It said some of the lines were from *The Color Purple* and some of the lines were from *Roots*, and it said the yams stuff was from *The Invisible Man*, but not the H. G. Wells novel where the man's actually invisible, and when Peggy woke me I remembered that yams bit and then all of a sudden I started thinking about sweet potatoes, because maybe I was still half dreaming, and then my mind was like: *I wonder if people eat sweet potato pie in Indiana?* and then I looked at the clock and I was like, "What the fuck, Peggy?"

She smacked the wall one more time. "It's time." Smack. "School." Smack again.

"You serious?" I said. I pulled my blankets all up on me. "I'm suspended, man."

"Suspended?"

"Means I can't go."

"I know what it means. Fucktard. You didn't tell me." She was wearing almost nothing, and she folded her arms I guess so I couldn't see her nipples poking through her shirt and her hair was in pigtails and, man, that just wasn't fair. "How long?"

"All week."

"The fuck you do?"

My eyes felt tight and I rubbed them. "Nothing really. Wrote something. Asked something. Said something. I dunno."

"Wrote something, asked something? So I got up for

nothing?" She threw up her arms, and it's weird being my age. "You didn't tell me not to wake you up."

"You do everything I don't tell you not to do?" And as soon as it left my mouth, I tried to understand what I'd said.

"What?" she said. "Nonsense-making little . . ." and I guess she wandered off to go back to sleep. But I always have a hard time sleeping once I'm up, and I just lay there thinking about Peggy. She's only six years older than me. I'm really not that young. My uncle is only twenty-eight. He took me on because if he did he got a monthly check. And I figured that was why I hadn't seen him for a few days—because he was off with my money getting high. He used to take my work money too. I worked at a grocery store as a bagger for a while, but when Uncle Joe didn't let me keep my checks I decided to get fired, because there's no point in working if you're not really getting paid. But my uncle's was the easiest place I'd ever lived. I had my own room. And he got me a phone. And if I got suspended a week no one seemed to care at all.

My room was still pretty dark, so I turned on my phone's flashlight, and I blasted Remote on the wall and kind of had him talk at me a bit, and after a while, I guess I was asleep again.

The next thing I remember was Bennet knocking on my window.

We live in the same apartment complex, Bennet and I, but he has a nicer unit because his mother's a nurse. She's always working. She's Bennet's white half, and she's ugly as hell, which I think means Bennet's daddy must have been a fucking god, because Bennet is one of the prettiest boys I've ever seen. Half-black people are usually good looking. Obama, Steph Curry, Halle Berry. Blake Griffin is an ugly motherfucker and Klay Thompson looks like an android. But Bennet looks like he'll find out he's gay while doing modeling and I'll see him on a poster someday, and I'll smile like crazy.

Straight guys will tell you they don't think about how other guys look, but that's a lie. I mean, ugly mother-fuckers can have lots of guy friends, but there's gotta be a kind of definition to their ugliness. They have to look like animals or super villains. But I've always preferred having handsome friends. And Bennet's funny too.

One time we went up to Kroger to get snacks, and we passed through the produce section and an old white woman with skin like a scrotum was setting carrots in her cart and Bennet asked her, "Ma'am, do you use your carrot tops?"

She looked at Bennet like he was batshit crazy. "Use them?"

"Not everyone does," said Bennet. "But I like good carrot tops."

She touched the curly, green carrot leaves. "How do you even?" she asked.

"The normal way."

"Normal?"

"If you ain't gonna use 'em, ma'am, and it's not too much my asking, do you mind if I take them off your hands? I mean if you're just gonna throw them out when you get home."

"Well . . ." she looked around like maybe she was being watched. "I guess that's fine."

And Bennet reached down and tore off the tops and walked them over to a roll of paper towels they had hanging there for customers to use, and he pulled off a piece, or a square or whatever you call it, and he began to twist up that carrot leaf in that paper towel like it was a joint. I mean, that's what it looked like. A joint the size of a baby's leg. And when it looked about as perfect as he could make it, he stuck it in his back pocket, put two fingers over his lips and shushed that old lady. Said, "Just between you and me." Said, "If I get caught, I won't tell anyone you gave it to me." And then we bought chips and ran about, and whenever one of us is feeling low we'll say, "Could go for some curly carrot leaf about now."

Also, Bennet is smart. Kid makes straight As. He's going to college for sure. Which is kinda crazy considering how much he loves dinking around on the internet.

When he came knocking at my window at about ten o'clock or something, the first thing he said when I pulled back the blinds and raised the glass was, "Lemme see your phone."

"Uh, good morning to you too, motherfucker."

"Father fucker." He winked, reached his hand inside. "Phone?" He grinned his pretty mouth at me.

And that's the thing about Bennet—he's too pretty to say no to. That old lady in the produce section probably even had the hots for him. Probably thought about him tearing off her curly carrot leaves when she was cooking those carrots. Probably simmered them in butter and tossed wild ideas about his half-black ass in the back of her mind.

Bennet crawled through my window and sat on a beanbag chair in the corner of my room, messed on my phone, and I pulled on pants, got ready for the day.

"You're smart, right?" I asked Bennet.

His eyes were lost in my phone, but he answered, "I guess."

"You read and shit?"

"'Bout as much as you."

"Yeah, but you read different shit. Have you read the black invisible man? The one that isn't invisible."

He looked up from the phone. "Is this like a riddle? The black invisible man that isn't black? How the fuck is he black then?"

"Nah, man. I don't think it's a riddle. It's why I'm asking."

"Like, *is water wet*?"

"What?"

"Is water wet?"

"Sure it is. Ain't it?"

Bennet googled something on my phone, waited for results, tapped a link with his pinky finger—because I'd watched him with my phone enough to know he scrolled with his right thumb and tapped links with his left pinky—and he held up the pointer finger of his left hand and read, "Water isn't wet. Wetness is a description of our experience of water; what happens to us when we come into contact with water in such a way that it impinges on our state of being. We, or our possessions, 'get wet.'"

"You're making *me* wet," I told him.

"Shit," he said.

"There's this invisible man that has something to do with Kendrick Lamar's yams."

His eyes tightened at me. "You're tripping."

I messed my hair in place and put on a hat. "Maybe," I said.

After I ate some breakfast—a handful of fake Cheerios—I asked Bennet what he wanted to do.

"This," he told me, and kind of held up my phone.

"All day?"

"All day."

I looked out the window. "Not me," I said. "It's supposed to be kinda nice." I missed the sun from South Texas. There, the sun shined like every day. We never really had winter. Our worst season was summer. It'd be over 100 degrees for three months in a row. At least it felt like it. And while I grumbled about that much sun when I was back home, now that I was being subjected to so many gray days, I missed it. When you have too much of something it begins to mean nothing to you. It was like when my mom and dad were alive. They'd come around and hug on me and I'd brush them away. Especially if I was in a bad mood. Like if they'd just had me clean my room or something. But if they came up and hugged me now, I'd be cool with it.

"I gotta get out in the sun if there is any," I told Bennet.

"How much data you got?"

Data was such a precious thing, man. My uncle let me have a phone, but he'd kick my ass if I went over my limit. It only happened once, and I didn't really fight back any.

He came into my room holding up a bill and said, "You've gone over."

"Huh?" I was in my beanbag chair.

"Your fucking limit, phone boy."

"Huh?"

Brian Allen Carr

"Huh me one more time and it's gonna be worse."

"Worse?"

"Fuck with a man's money and you get hands."

"Hands?"

My uncle dropped the bill and picked up his fists. He smiled. "Just a good-natured ass-kicking."

That was the thing about my uncle. It must've been why Peggy loved him. Even when he was being a dick, he seemed lovable. He kicked my ass that day chuckling the whole time. "Gonna go over data again?" He smiled at me.

"Nah." My nose was bleeding.

He jabbed my ribs twice more and then gave me a hug and kissed my cheek. I could smell his hot-alcohol breath, his Axe body spray. "Damn, nephew, you took that good." Then he gave me a beer, and we arm wrestled and he let me win.

Bennet tapped a few things on my phone. "You got plenty of data," he said.

We made to leave out the front door but on the way out Peggy stopped me. "Where you going?"

"Out."

"No shit, but where?"

"No exact destination."

"I can't find your fucking uncle."

"You text him?"

"Texted. Called. Facebook messaged. Tweeted at."
She had her phone and was scrolling on it. "Like he just
dropped off the face of the earth."

"I mean, yeah. That's Uncle Joe." He was in and out.
He was there and gone. Dragging through life the
way he did.

Peggy looked at selfie view on her phone and messed
with an eyelash. "I know where he was on Saturday and I
know where he was supposed to be yesterday."

"So what's the big deal? He'll be around soon. This
afternoon or tomorrow."

Peggy messed with her lip, still in selfie mode. "If he's
not back by tomorrow, I'll officially be worried. Right
now I'm concerned. Rent's up on Friday. And that's when
it's up up. That's the latest we can pay. So unless you find
your uncle or eight hundred dollars . . ."

"You want me to give you eight hundred dollars?"

"I want someone to."

"If I gave you eight hundred dollars, what would you
give me?" I lifted my chin toward her.

"A place to stay."

"I guess I'll keep my eyes open then."

We got outside and Bennet was like, "Smooth, struggler."

"She thinks I'm too young."

"You are too young."

"Nah. Age is a number. You get to a certain age, you've got all the magic you'll ever have."

"Hopefully you haven't reached that age yet."

"Fuck you, struggler."

Now, let me take a minute to explain the word *struggler*, because it's an important word to me and only me. It's my word. Mine and Erika's. She's my friend from back on the border. Mexican as they come. Calls herself Latina. And Chicana. And other shit I can't remember.

Anyhow, she was my best friend down there since I got there in fifth grade. I was ten and I hadn't grown up on the border, so my Spanish was nothing. I mean, I really didn't know anything beyond *hola*, and on the first day I was in math class, a few of the kids started calling me *güero*. And I'd heard that, except when Mexicans say it they say "wed-O" and when white people say it they say "where-O," but either way it's basically like "white boy." But it's weird, because you can use it good and you can use it bad. Well, I guess the word *Mexican* is like that too. And the word *Jew*. And the word *black*. But with güero it's more complicated than that. But it's not as complicated as the N-word. Cause like, with the N-word, it can mean like the absolute best and the absolute worst. Güero can only mean kinda bad or kinda good.

Let me give you an example.

If you see a white boy, and you don't like him, and your

tone is a bit flat, and you say "güero," it's kinda like you just called him fucker.

But you can have a friend who is a light-skinned Mexican, and if you call him güero it's kind of a term of endearment. Like honey. Or blondie. Or slick.

These kids weren't calling me honey, or blondie, or slick. They were calling me güero.

I was the only white kid in the class, and that had never happened to me before. I was nervous, and I didn't want to feel nervous. Before I went to school I was like, "Blend in. Be cool." But my mind kept racing.

I didn't blend. I froze. I went to school and I felt the strangest sensation. I felt like I had wandered into an alternative world. It seemed that everybody noticed me. And while that's probably how it feels the first day of any new school, it was worse, because I felt so different.

I probably seemed like fresh fish at jail. You could probably taste my fear like skunk stink. And then some of the kids started calling me güero, and that's when Erika took up for me. She spit some lickety-split Spanish at the other kids in class, and when the kids quit teasing me, she extended her hand and we were introduced.

She told me all about how she had lived a few years in Michigan and how back there her role was reversed. She was different than everyone else. And how she had been teased, and how she had a friend stick up for her.

"Hannah," Erika said, "that was her name. And she wouldn't let anyone say anything rude to me, and I'll never see her again but I'll never forget her."

Erika kind of took care of me. She taught me how to not feel weird on the border. She took me to parties and teased me like I was just a person rather than a white person, and it got to where I don't think we thought of each other as anything other than friends. I mean not really. We'd tease each other for being what we were—white/Mexican—but we might as well have teased each other for being too short or too tall or redheaded. I hope I see her again, but who knows.

She asked me that first day, "You a smuggler or a struggler?"

"What?" I said.

"All the whites that come to the border are either drug smugglers or life strugglers."

I thought about that a minute. "I've never smuggled anything," I said.

"Struggler it is," Erika said, and she stuck out her tongue and blew a raspberry at me.

I've noticed that anyone who hangs out with me awhile picks up the word, and Bennet hangs out with me the most.

My apartment door nearly opened on to the playground, so we stepped out and sat on the swings, but I was a bit wrong about the weather. It was nice out, but it wasn't sunny. It was a harsh winter, my Indiana friends told me. We had gotten a few days off from school because of snow and a few other days school started late, and that morning was in the thirties, which just then felt like heaven. In Texas, that would've seemed cold as hell, but I guess I'd gotten used to things.

"So much for sun," said Bennet. The swing set chains winced and chirped.

"More like a good day for a movie."

"*Black Panther* is out."

"Is it?"

"Just this weekend. I gotta see it in the theater."

"Shit, let's go." I stood from the saddle of the swing.

Bennet always seemed to have allowance and he was good about sharing. I guess that was our thing. He'd borrow my phone and I'd borrow his cash. "How?" Bennet said. "If we go to the theater, they'll probably call the truancy officers."

"They will not. Just act like you belong there. We'll tuck in our shirts and we won't wear hats. That works every time."

"That might work for you, but they're not letting a black teenager into the movies on a Monday during school."

Around that time I heard Peggy come out of the

apartment with her keys in her hand. She spotted us and hollered over, "What you guys doing?"

"Thinking about going to a movie," I told her.

"Movie?" said Peggy, and she walked toward us, her keys going clink, clink, clang.

"You heard of 'em? Picture stories that they show in the dark."

"Like a date?" she said. "You gonna share popcorn?"

I looked at Bennet.

"See," said Peggy. "I can be an asshole too. Look for your uncle."

"Instead of the movie?"

"On the way to the movie," said Peggy, "the way home. Text some of those numbnuts he tags with."

Then Bennet looked up. "Be honest," he said. "If we go to a movie they'll call the cops on me, huh?"

Peggy regarded him. "Shave your head. We got clippers. Have Riggle take you down to a zero. You look white with no hair."

Bennet sort of scowled at her. "When you ever see me without hair?"

"In my imagination." She walked off to her car with her keys jangling on. "Look for your uncle," she hollered back at us before hopping behind the wheel and driving away.

Bennet looked at me. "You think I should make myself look as white as possible to go see *Black Panther*?"

"You wanna see it?"

He rubbed his head. "Yeah, motherfucker."

Shaving a boy's head is getting close to a boy. You have to be gentle with their scalp and hold down their ears. We set up shop in my bathroom and I had Bennet take off his shirt. He didn't have any hair on his chest, and when he leaned over for me to get the back of his head, I could see the bumps of his spine. He got cold and he got goose pimples. The clippers hummed and purred.

"Tssss," said Bennet, when I guess I nicked him once. "Watch it with those filthy things."

"They ain't filthy."

"Man, look around."

I turned the clippers off, and Bennet had half a head of hair. I'd gotten the left side, but the right side was still fluffy, right down the middle of his scalp. Half sandpaper, half Brillo pad. We made eye contact in the mirror and the shaved side of him already looked white. My eyes went this way, that. A sort of dust-haze hung in the jittery fluorescent light. A veil of scag sweat clung to the mirror. Heaps of gunk and stray hairs were here and there on the surfaces. Water stains. Soap scum. Piles of lint.

I flipped the clippers back on. "Be nice or I'll leave you that way."

Bennet frowned at his half-haired reflection. "I'm nice," he said. "I'm sweet as pie."

When I was done, I toweled him up, flipped on Peggy's blow-dryer and blow-dried him clean.

We both looked him over good after he threw on his shirt and tucked it in. He stiffened his posture, pursed his lips like a duck, looked at himself in the mirror. "I would like to purchase a single ticket for the next showing of the feature film *Black Panther*," he said. He shrugged at his reflection.

"White as fuck," I told him.

I don't want to spoil the movie for you. Or Bennet. I mean, he watched most of it, but a lot of the time he played on my phone. I don't get why people do that. We sat in the far back row so he could phone it up. We had started in the dead center of the theater, but during the previews I got the sense that he was gonna have the phone out the whole time, and I didn't want to ruin the movie for everyone else, so I made him move with me. And he was like, "Oh, I gotta sit in the back, huh?"

And I was like, "If you're playing with my phone you do."

Some people don't do movie theater etiquette. On the other hand, some people treat it like church. Erika would shush everyone in the theaters. She'd stand up and glare at people. I'm sort of in the middle. I mean, I love movies. And I love seeing them in theaters best of all. It's the smell, really. Or the darkness. There's a kind of carbonated taste to everything. A buttery gloss from the acres and acres of popcorn that have passed through. A sweet reek of syrup from the vast gallons of soda. Sticky floors. Springy seat cushions. The speakers thrumming your bones.

I will say: the big screen is the only way to see *Black Panther*. It starts slow, and I would like to see Michael B. Jordan make it through a full movie alive. And Bennet thought it was weird that the bad guy was African American while the good guy was African African. But from the time when T'Challa was tossed over the waterfall until the end, it was one of the better action movies I'd seen.

It wasn't as good as people were saying—because people were saying it was the most perfect movie of all time—but it was solid, and I could see why people were getting bent out of shape over it.

Black folks on the internet were acting like it was a religious event, and white folks on the internet were acting like it was a sign of the apocalypse, but the only way it could have been either of those things is if it was both of those things in equal measure and the noise of it being so important in opposite directions just made it average out to being just a movie.

When the flick was over, we walked back into the day, and sun had broken open the clouds.

That's one of the things that Indiana had better than Texas: it has the most dramatic skies. These sort of clogs of gray storm fronts, these sort of clumps of white pillow clouds. Every shade from black to white passing through purple, through blue. With these yellow stains, these glowing edges from the sun's rays. That many colors in one spot is dizzying.

In Texas, the sky is blue-menthol and white. Pale the way chalk is pale. Flatter than glass.

"Shit," said Bennet, as we made our way across the rain-slicked parking lot. "You're out of data?"

"What?"

He handed me back my phone. "Out."

I thumbed some stuff closed, looked at my settings. I covered my eyes with my hair. "It's only the nineteenth."

"Yeah but it's a short month."

I was happy for that. I needed a new month. It was my second winter in Indiana, but it was my first bad one. I had moved up the January before, and back then everyone had warned me that winters got worse, and they all seemed to use "the blizzard of '78" as the kind of measuring stick to rate all winters against. The winter I was in, the 2018 one, didn't compare to that, I was told. But to my Texas-raised ass, it was the grayest and coldest I'd known.

Everything seemed compressed by the cold, weighted by colorlessness. Sunlight appeared charcoal filtered. The ground was wet with winter. Ice melt glistened or snow patches grew dirt stained and muddled. Dead leaves clumped in frozen heaps. All the streets were salted.

I once got high after about a foot of accumulation. I walked around in the sun-sparkling snow—one of the few days the sky was crystal clear—and in my highness, the snow seemed like beach sand. I was bundled and gloved. I was hooded and wool-socked. I traipsed in the virgin snow like I was plowing through dunes, like I was on the national seashore, like I was at South Padre Island.

That was one of the only happy winter days I'd known that season. The grayness dampened my heart. The coldness made me pout and whine.

So, on February 19th, with the magic, stormy sky above me, I felt a great burden shrug away. February *was* short. And I thought winter was ending. And I had just seen the most polarizing action movie ever made, and the next day I didn't have to go to school.

"What do you want to do now?" I asked Bennet.

"I gotta get home. Before Mom does. Wanna walk with me back to the apartment?"

"Nah, man. I'm gonna look for my uncle, I guess."

"Where?"

"We go to a place sometimes."

"Alright then."

"Alright." I watched Bennet walk away.

My uncle was my mother's brother. Is my mother's brother? I'm not sure how to say it. He was, at a time, her little brother. Now . . .

I don't think he knew her well though. They were ten years apart, and my mom left Indiana for Texas when she was eighteen, but there was an old cemetery atop a hill in a park near downtown, and my uncle remembered my mother taking him there, and when I first got to Opioid, Indiana, we went there and sat on Ima Schort's tombstone and we drank hot coffee from a thermos, and my uncle smoked a Swisher Sweet.

"Funny name, huh?" He had a smoke-coarsened voice and an addict-thin frame. He looked like he'd kick a dog and give you the shirt off his back. He had an angular face that gave you the impression he was always paying attention even when he was fucked up and his mind was miles away. I've got a face like that too. So did Mom. But

I don't have Uncle Joe's smile. "This town was almost called Schortville," my uncle said, and nudged me. "On account of her family. We would've all been Schorties. Or something. How they name people from a city. Like New Yorkers."

"Or Houstonians," I said.

"Exactly," he said. "We would've been Schorties."

I think we both kind of thought about that, because it got quiet.

Then my uncle said, "Your mother was a good old girl. I'm sorry she's gone. Hell, I was sorry when she left here." He sort of waggled to shift his posture. "But I guess I always figured she'd be back."

I sipped coffee. "She's been gone awhile," I said. She died when I was nine and I was sixteen when we were at the cemetery.

"Yeah, but we ain't talked about it."

We had seen each other at her funeral, but he was very much a stranger to me then, and we'd only talked about race cars that day. I've never known anything about racing, and I never will know anything about racing, but he would talk to me about drivers as though they were A-list celebrities, and he would talk to me about racing events as though they were national holidays.

"Thanks for taking me in," I told my uncle as we sat there on the tombstones. My coffee breath hit the cold air as steam and dragged away like tissues caught in the wind.

My uncle blew smoke rings. "Don't fuck it up," he said.

I walked from the theater straight to the cemetery hoping to find—I'm not sure what. Maybe I thought my uncle would be curled in a stupor, his back against Ima's ancient grave. The first time I'd gone there with him, he said that he'd spend time there on low days.

"When I fuck up," he said, "I come here. Have a smoke. Think about your grandfather. Think about your mom. It's not that I remember her all that well, but I remember that I wish I knew her better, y'know? I wish I called more or that she called me. I'd heard she was struggling after your father died. I didn't reach out, but I was young. Like, twenty. That probably seems like an adult age to you now, but it's not. Hell, I'm nearly thirty and I don't feel like an adult yet."

But that morning, the cemetery was empty. I sat on a tombstone that belonged to one of Opioid, Indiana's founders for an hour or so watching the sun shred the clouds with its rays. All the tree limbs were stripped by weather and looked like insect antennae or cracks in glass. I didn't have any data, so all my messages sent as SMS. Peggy still hadn't heard anything. I kept tracing Ima's name with my finger and thinking: *Schorties. Schorties. Schorties.* I wanted to google Ima but couldn't. To see what she was all about. To see what had brought the Schorts here and from where. I can't imagine traveling in old times. In wagons for months. To say goodbye forever to your loved ones and head west into mysterious terrain. Drinking river water. Cooking on campfires. Shitting in the bushes miles from anywhere. Building a house when you got where you were going with boards that you made. Out of trees that you felled. I could never do anything that berserk.

When I got bored of pondering, I decided to go home.

Peggy was dressed when I got back, but she wasn't wearing shoes. Her hair was out of its pigtails and wet and she didn't have on makeup and it looked like she'd been licking her lips for hours.

"Still nothing?" I asked. Her eyes were surprised when I opened the door.

"Nope." She licked her lips.

"Can I borrow your phone for like five minutes?"

"Where's yours?"

"I'm out of data."

"'Cause of all the porn you watch." Lick.

"I don't watch porn."

"The walls are paper-thin. I can hear everything."

"Fine I watch porn. But I won't on your phone, I just wanna look someone up."

"Tough. I'm waiting to hear back from folks."

"Whatever," I told her.

I went to my bedroom and lay on my bed. I had a book about philosophy that I found on a discard cart the library put out. I read about this old philosopher called Diogenes. He was a cynic. He lived in a barrel. He pissed everyone off.

One time he got caught masturbating in public but he said there was nothing wrong with it. He said masturbation was amazing. He said he wished he could stop his hunger by rubbing his belly, the way he could stop his lust by rubbing his cock.

Tuesday

On Tuesday morning, when I woke up, Peggy was gone and the apartment was dead silent. I like being alone. I think some people need people and want to be around others at all times, but I think orphans get to the point where they prefer their own thoughts. Don't get me wrong, if Mom walked through the front door, I'd do anything with her she wanted to do. Some people get mad at their parents when they off themselves, but me, I understood. My dad was her world, I guess. He died when I was six. He was a trucker and he crashed, and for three years Mom struggled along in life. She stared at the walls when we were eating dinner, and sometimes she'd cry for no reason and she couldn't really hold a job at all, because she always had to call in sick. She'd lay in bed tossing and turning. But even when she was as bad as she got, we would always do Remote. We'd lay in bed, warm against each other. Sometimes her hair would fall on my face. And I'd watch across the room for Remote on the wall. His voice coming out of my mother's mouth. The two of them separate but tied together.

Here's how Remote told me Tuesday got its name:

When the Earthlings realized that every day was its own thing, they decided that different events should happen on different days, but they weren't certain if that was practical. They came to Remote with their problem, and I thought about it. "What is the least predictable endeavor of man?" I asked, and they agreed that war was the least likely to operate on a fixed schedule.

"Still," they said, "it would be nice if war could take place one day a week."

"And it would be nice," another suggested, *"if that day was early in the week, but not the first day of the week. I've noticed,"* he said, *"that I'm pretty sluggish on Mondays. And fighting wars when you're sluggish is the worst."*

So, Remote sent for Tues, who was the greatest warrior amongst Earthlings, to seek his council on the matter.

"Wage an entire war in a single day?" Tues said when the Earthlings expressed their plan.

"Is it not feasible?" I asked.

Tues had a pipe that he smoked, and he could blow the smoke into elaborate configurations. He took a deep puff of his pipe, and he exhaled a battlefield and on the field, smoke soldiers met and killed one another until the smoke dissipated and the room was once again still. "Perhaps," Tues said. "It will require experimentation."

He corralled his armies and they devised a plan. For an entire week, they would wake each morning and start a war with a new nation. If they completed a war in a single day, the Earthlings would know that everything could be compartmentalized and organized thusly.

There was so much death, my word.

Tues's armies were proficient and skilled, and

their opponents were caught entirely off guard. The armies would commit their acts of aggression, and lay into the resting nations, slaying many before the warfare was even realized.

Still, after a week of fighting, Tues's army had yet to topple a nation in a single day.

"It just takes more time than that," Tues said.

Remote was discouraged. "We must devise another way," I said.

Tues took a great puff of his pipe, and he blew smoke in the shape of regular smoke, and all the elders watched it to see what it might become.

"That was just smoke," one of the Earthlings said.

"I noticed," said Tues, "that my men fought better than they ever had, on these one-day campaigns. Because they thought they would only be fighting one-day wars. In a sense," Tues said, "they were. In another sense, we've been fighting for seven straight days. And all of those wars shared a common goal. The goal of determining how quickly a conflict could be resolved. Those are probably all parts of the same conflict."

Remote liked this kind of talking. Remote likes speeches that are really just thoughts thought out loud.

"You think it's best to tell people wars will only last a day?" I asked.

"I think it's best to tell people all things will only last a day. That every night should be the end of something, and every morning should be the start of something else, even if it isn't entirely true."

Remote loved this idea, and for his help in this matter, I named the second day of the week Tuesday after Tues, and I also decided that we would call language that says one thing but means another "blowing smoke" on account of Tues and his pipe and his magical smoking.

It was about eleven before I finally got going. I loafed around and watched TV. I played hacky sack in the living room and ate a half-dozen eggs. I like making omelettes. My mom showed me how to make them before she died.

And I made one of them for Peggy once, and she said that some restaurants used omelettes as job applications. Like, if you wanted to be a cook at a good place, the chef would watch you make an omelette and if you did it well, you got the job.

"I could go up to McDonald's and make them an omelette and get hired on?" I said to her.

We were sitting in the kitchen and Uncle Joe was

on the sofa in the adjacent room, and he was wasted on something, and he kept humming a tune that sounded like Japanese music.

"Not McDonald's, you fucking idiot." Peggy smiled at me. "*McDonald's*. No, a real restaurant."

"Like which one?"

"Hell, I don't even know if we've got one in Opioid, Indiana."

This was around the time I got fired from the grocery store, and money was tight, I guess, because no one was working.

Peggy lit a cigarette. "Someone around here needs a fucking job." She blew smoke at Uncle Joe. "He's too *important* to follow schedules."

Here's how making an omelette works. First, you crack three or four eggs into a bowl. It depends on the size of your pan. You have to crack the perfect amount, and it kind of takes trial and error to figure out what's best. Then you set your pan on the stove and turn it to medium-high. The best pans are new nonstick. The second-best pans are cast-iron skillets. The third-best pans are old nonstick. If you don't have one of those three pans, you can't make a good omelette.

While the pan is heating, you scramble the eggs. You use a fork. Some people use whisks, but that is overkill. The trick is you have to scramble the hell out of the eggs. I mean, you scramble them until they're scrambled and then you scramble them some more. They've got to be totally mixed up. Sometimes, if you don't do it long enough, you can tell what part of the eggs were whites and what part of the eggs were yolks, but when you're making an omelette, it has to be an absolute mystery.

I like using butter for omelettes. Some people use oil. Whatever you use, you have to use a lot of it.

Once I stayed in a hotel with my old guardian, and there was a breakfast buffet and there was a chef there in a white jacket who was cooking omelettes to order.

"We call this an action station," the chef told me. And the way he made omelettes was he cooked everything that was in my omelette and then he added the eggs. But to me that's just a kind of scrambled eggs. Egg mush. Jumbled up.

I think the best omelettes are just eggs with maybe cheese in it but that's it, because that's how Mom taught me to make them, and she told me it was the color and the shape that determined if they were really good. There was supposed to be no color from the cooking, no brown. The eggs were supposed to be pale yellow when cooked, and the omelettes were supposed to be shaped like footballs.

I never cooked the eggs when Mom was alive. Not really. I'd crack the eggs and scramble the eggs, and I'd pour the eggs into the pan, but Mom always did the cooking part.

It works like this: you pour the eggs and they should hiss slightly when they land. They should sound like the letter *S* when you whisper the word *sweetie*. Not like the letter *S* when you say the word *STOP*. Then you use a spatula to move the eggs constantly until they set up enough from the heat and the moving to leave them be.

This is kinda gross, but it's like playing with a booger. I mean, sometimes you pick your nose and what comes out is a fully formed, flickable booger, and you can just flip your finger and the thing will fly away. But sometimes you pick your nose and a strand of goo comes out, and no matter how much you flip your finger it just stays clung to you. So, what do you do? You move the thing between your fingers—right, between the pads of your thumb and your pointer—until it's like cooked enough that it becomes its own thing. It no longer just sticks to you.

I can't remember if that's how Mom told me to think of it, or if I just realized that later on. But once all the eggs are the consistency of a flickable booger, you pick up the pan and tap the bottom of it a few times on the burner so the skin of the omelette settles down on the pan. Then you count to eight. After that, you fold it by a third. Like you would a letter for an envelope. Then you count to ten. Then you slide the egg onto a plate, folding it the rest of the way as it falls.

The first omelette I made that Tuesday morning I didn't do very good, so I made another one that was perfect, and I even said, "Look, Mom, I'm a breakfast chef," when the thing slid onto the plate.

And then I thought: *maybe I should be a cook.* I mean, when that sheet went around and I filled it out and said that I wanted to be either Autistic Ross or the Bicycling Confederate, it was a joke, but the joke was really on me, because I had no idea what I wanted to do with myself. When you're an orphan, you don't really have goals—or at least no one is there to give them to you. Everything anyone suggests to you seems so logical it's demeaning. I wanna be a dreamer, dammit. I wanna look off at sunshine and think up fantasy jobs to do for myself. All the counselors and guardians are like, "You like puzzles, be an electrician. You like art, paint houses." I don't know what my father wanted me to be and I don't think my mom really wanted me to be a cook. She just wanted to teach me how to make eggs. She didn't work until my dad died, and even then she was in and out of jobs. Dad was a truck driver but I doubt he would've wanted me to do that. Especially after he got killed driving.

Mom and I used to have this map on the refrigerator that we would use to follow his route. We would mark where he was on a dry-erase board that had a picture of America on it. We even had a special marker. It's one of those memories that seem like dreams. That have parts of memories in them that couldn't be. Because I remember, one time, we were marking his route on the map, and then my mom looked at me and said, "Guess who's home?" and then she opened up the refrigerator and my father crawled out of it.

But there's no way that happened.

And don't get me wrong. I figured the skills my mother gave me wouldn't be worth a sock full of dicks if I lurked up to some restaurant and smiled into the kitchen asking to talk to the chef. In my experience you had to fill out an application and then talk to a manager, and then talk to another manager and then maybe do a quiz. I knew some kids who cooked up at McDonald's, but what they did didn't sound like cooking to me at all. It sounded like putting stuff places.

But Mom never told me what she thought I should be. And one day Dad didn't come back from his route. The dry-erase America just clung to the refrigerator with a mark on it that started out where we lived and ended in the last spot we talked to him before he ran off the road.

After that Mom didn't really talk to me when she made eggs. And she would stare off at nothing when we ate breakfast. And she would shuffle me to the car to take me to school. And she would barely say anything to me when she picked me up.

And then one day she didn't wake me up. I sat up in my bed and the house was quiet and I called to her. But I didn't hear anything, and there was a stiffness to her not hollering back for me. Like every part of that house was listening along with me for a voice that wouldn't come, and like every part of that house was disappointed or worried. Like when you open a present at Christmas and it's not what you wanted. That still. The ceiling fan was paralyzed where it hung above me. The light seemed like plastic. I dragged out of bed and went down the hallway to her room. Her lights and fan were on. She was covered with blankets. I crawled on her bed, but when I touched her she didn't feel right.

I finished eating my second omelette and decided to catch a shower. I had big plans. I was either gonna find a real restaurant, my uncle, or the Bicycling Confederate. I figured I'd let the universe decide for me, because I can never find the thing I'm looking for. I always find the thing I was looking for last.

Let me explain.

Let's say I lose my hat. And I'm looking all over the apartment but can't find it. I mean, I've looked in the bathroom and my room. And my uncle's bathroom and his room. And my closet. And his closet. And the kitchen. And even in the freezer—because sometimes you just do weird shit. And on the back of the sofa. On top of the TV. On the tables. On the desks. In the nooks and in the corners.

If I finally say "fuck it," and just decide to go out without a hat on, I'll somehow realize I can't find my phone.

This happens to me all the time. I can't remember where anything is. It gets to be where I cuss at myself and want to die, because I can't believe how forgetful one person can be. I mean, is this the best God can do? This creation that I am of his? That's what I always wonder. Is this just how it works? You think you need all these things you have, but where the fuck are they?

Now, I can go out without my hat, sure. But I can't leave without my phone. Who can? What do you even do? You can't text people to meet up. You can't look up shit on the internet. If you need directions you gotta ask some milky-eyed stranger and they either never know the way or have like crazy landmarks they want you to look for. Old trees. Orange station wagons. At the burnt-down condominium hang a left. If you get to the spotted hooting owl with two left wings you've gone too far.

So, I start looking everywhere for my phone. All the

usual places. In the bathroom and my room. And my uncle's bathroom and his room. And my closet. And his closet. And the kitchen. And even in the freezer. And on the back of the sofa. On top of the TV. On the tables. On the desks. In the nooks and in the corners.

Then: bam!

I find my fucking hat.

That's how it always works for me, so I figured if I went out and looked for a real restaurant maybe my uncle would turn up.

But you know what happened?

I walked a block toward downtown, and the damn Bicycling Confederate was swerving down the road, his flag flap, flapping like a motherfucking ceremony was going on somewhere. Like this cat had been sent home years ago when the Civil War ended and he'd just been taking his sweet time getting there.

Did they have bicycles then? I was out of data and couldn't check or risk an ass-kicking when my uncle finally turned up.

And I'll be honest, when I saw the Bicycling Confederate it did me a number, because I'd sort of put him on the back burner of my brain. Back with the widowed socks and old condom wrappers. I'd never had sex, but I'd tried on scads of condoms. And I didn't know how to approach him. He was a few hundred yards up from me, I guess. At least a football field. But his flag was unmistakable, and his gait—well if he'd been walking it would've been his gait—was for certain. Like spotting a goose flying from the ground. Long-ass neck and wings going flippity. This crazy struggler with his wrists rested on the handlebars and his slow back and forth, side to side. How he never got hit by cars was one of the miracles of the universe.

I thought: *How the hell do you follow a bicyclist on foot?* He was slow, but he wasn't *walking* slow. And I'm in shape, but I'm not in long-distance-running shape.

He was up on Main Street and I feel like if I'm going to tell you any more of this story I have to explain to you what Opioid, Indiana, is like and how it's shaped and who the hell lives here.

Now, in Texas all the history is drenched in war. They always say there's been "six flags over Texas." There's a theme park in Texas named after the slogan. First there was Spain and then there was France and then there was Mexico and then there was the Republic of Texas. Then the United States. Then the Confederacy. Then the United States again. So, it's really seven but I guess we either don't count the Confederacy or pretend we're not really part of the United States. And I'm sure you could find millions of motherfuckers to gladly take up either stance on the matter.

Most of those transitions involved bloody battles. The most famous of these was the Alamo in San Antonio, which I went to on my first ever vacation. We walked around the mission and I stuck my fingers in a bunch of bullet holes, and Mom and Dad were still alive then, and they stuck their fingers in bullet holes too. But anytime you drive anywhere in Texas you see signs marking skirmishes and ambushes and battles galore. It's probably all a bit exaggerated, but that is the Texas way.

In Indiana, they never fought over shit. I learned that in school. Indiana history is the history of home building. Crop rotations. Outstanding winters. Their legends are of regular people—men who were strong enough to lift a wheelbarrow one-handed, women who could bake swell sugar cream pies. There's some basketball players. Horse racers. Kurt Vonnegut. So it goes.

To be remembered in Texas you have to die in a coonskin cap after murdering a half thousand men single-handed. You have to become a president or be Beyoncé or Wes Anderson. Or Willie Nelson. Or the rapper Scarface.

There's a highway in Indianapolis named after a musician called Babyface, and all his most famous songs were performed by other people.

That's Indiana, though. Hoosiers are some behind-the-scenes motherfuckers.

Even Larry Bird, who is their most famous athlete,

is most famous for being white. He's an American man. Famous for being white. He *is* Indiana.

Opioid is a good enough place, but if you called it rinky-dink, you wouldn't be a liar. There's a courthouse downtown that they decorate for the seasons. There's a cemetery everyone jogs through, and everybody feels safe there, like the corpses might come out and have a picnic and cheer you on. There's a college. There's a river. There's a hotel with a bar in it. In the evenings, if you stand still in the road, you can hear old men whistling Cole Porter songs. That dude was from Indiana. His childhood home was turned into a meth lab.

So, the Bicycling Confederate was down Main toward the courthouse, and I watched him pedal up that direction, and I decided I could lollygag a bit, and that I could most likely perch up on the courthouse lawn and maybe watch the dude ride around the square.

I wasn't trying to draw attention to myself. I figured if I sprinted to him he might see me coming and get nervous and race away, or a cop would see me running and get suspicious and want to talk. My shirt was tucked in, and I didn't have a hat on, but you can only go so far before you look like a kid. You ever seen a grown man sprinting in regular clothes on an afternoon for no reason? It's a bad look. Seems like they're on drugs.

Also, if I broke a sweat, there was no way I could get a

job making omelettes if I found a real restaurant. I didn't have realistic expectations of landing any real work that day, but if I had pit stains on a 30-degree Tuesday, and I showed up when I was supposed to be at school, I sure as shit wasn't going to get hired.

In Texas, you come to understand the size of an acre. Maybe it's lots of places. But in Texas, people are always saying how many acres a thing is, and the courthouse in Opioid, Indiana, sits on like 2.6 acres, if I had to guess, and around it there is a square with businesses that face toward the courthouse at the center. It's like an old-fashioned town. From back when people wanted to see other people. I wonder what towns will look like in the future. Towns that get designed after the internet. Tunnels with phone chargers everywhere, I bet.

Now, if you go out of town a mile, you're in cornfields, and so I wonder what Opioid was like in the 1800s. It must've seemed like it had sprung out of the crops. Like the citizens of the place had gotten lost in a corn maze and just decided to build. They didn't know that if you're in a labyrinth, if you put your hand on the right wall and never let go, and just move forward forever, you'll eventually get free.

Geese that probably should have flown south for winter dawdled on the courthouse lawn in weird little packs. They had black heads and white cheeks and they spread their wings at passersby, squawking at everyone like a bully would.

That day was only sort of gray. There are different levels to the grayness. I mean, back home there are different levels to the sunshine too, but you can't contemplate the differences or else you'll go blind. You can stare at gray for forever. You can look up at the sky and widen your eyes like you do with those 3D posters and start seeing the secret shit God puts in there.

I was thinking up a metaphor to decide how to best explain it, and I decided it worked best to use coffee, because at the grocery store where I had worked, there was a coffee bar that shoppers stopped at before moving through their lists, and I learned about all the different ways coffee could be served to you.

Here's what I came up with:

Creamy - That's when the clouds are kind of white. You can't see any blue. Can't see the sun, but you know it isn't gonna start raining. And every so often, you spot a shadow on the ground. You could even make Remote and talk to him if you got real lonely.

Decaf - You can't see the sun. Can't see the blue. And you might catch a sprinkle. Who knew? No shadows at all. All the colors look like they've been made from clay.

Half caf - Gray. Dark. Maybe gonna be raining in a minute. Colors look like they are covered in film.

Coffee - The clouds look like they are annihilating the color blue. And it's not raining, but there is just water in the air. I guess you could call it misting. But that doesn't seem right. Because I feel like when it's misting it seems like mist is falling. But when Indiana weather is coffee, there is a drop of rain dispersed in every breath you take.

Espresso - It feels like you can chew the gray. Like if you moved your hand fast enough, you could grab a patch of gray and put it in an envelope and mail it off to a pen pal so they could always have a piece of Indiana. You can't tell if the air is wet or not, because that would imply some kind of dryness in the air to measure it against. If you stay outside long enough, you have to change your clothes or dry them by a fire.

I sat in the decaf day amongst the geese watching the Bicycling Confederate do circles around the courthouse, his flag whipping mildly behind him, the off-red and blue of it like something a kid would design in art class. And I sort of pondered the way other people considered him, watching the people in cars look at him as he did his left turns, and I didn't see anyone really furious at his flag and that kind of boggled me.

I tried to contemplate other symbols that would be comparable and what reactions they might get, but it's complicated.

Lots of people compare the Confederate flag to the Nazi flag, but that's not quite right. The Nazis did things for the first time. They set up shop in a country and did murderous things that had never been done before, but the Confederates just wanted to do what the country had always done. I mean, they were wrong, but at a point in time, so was everybody.

Because, here's something, New York had slavery longer than Texas did. Did you know that? New York had slavery from the time it was founded in 1624 to 1830. I saw some dood on Twitter who lived in New York calling some states "slave states." And I was like: Well what were the slave states?

And I think these are the only states that never had slavery: Ohio, Indiana, Illinois, Michigan, Iowa, Wisconsin, Minnesota, Nevada, California, Oregon and Kansas. But I read for a long time and I really couldn't tell. I mean, not all the other states were proud about having slavery.

When you're a kid from Texas, you try to figure these things out. The adults can't explain it to you. The adults can't explain shit.

In a few months, when I turn eighteen, I have to register for the military draft. But the military draft is illegal. You can get way more fucked up on alcohol than you can on weed, and only one of those is legal. These days, when you go see a doctor, there's a decent chance you'll leave pain-free but addicted. And Coca-Cola still has coca leaf in it.

That shit is for real. I know Coca-Cola's whole history.

The drink that it's based on was from Europe. It had red wine and cocaine. People drank it to get their swerve on. The guy who made up Sherlock Holmes was a fan of the old kind of Coke, and the guy who wrote *Journey to the Center of the Earth* imbibed it too. So, I guess the stuff was good for writing on and fucking on, and Pope Leo XIII used it to talk to God.

The guy who started Coca-Cola was a morphine addict. He had been a Confederate soldier and got wounded and hooked on painkillers they gave him. But he didn't want to be a morphine addict anymore.

Listen, I've seen opioid addicts. They can't do shit but get fucked up. They lie in heaps just thinning their eyes at the universe. Their faces look to be contemplating heaps of ash. Like they're sleepy around a campfire.

So, this guy figured out a new drug to do. A drug that made him more zippy than loopy but that still made him feel good. He drank wine mixed with coca leaves. Then, in the county where they made it, alcohol was made illegal. So they took the wine out and replaced it with sugar water.

At first, you could only buy Coke in a pharmacy. When they learned how to bottle it, black people, who couldn't go inside the pharmacy because of Jim Crow laws, started drinking the stuff. This made people worried that black doods would start getting coked up and raping white girls. Coca-Cola decided to pull the coca out to make the racist customers happy.

Except, they didn't really. To this day Coca-Cola ships in millions and millions of dollars' worth of coca leaves every year and they turn it into something called "Merchandise Number 5," and that's a secret ingredient in the formula.

I think they're the only company in the US that sells illegal drugs in some modified form AND sponsors the Olympics.

But, right, if you get busted with a dime bag of cocaine, you can't tell the cops that it's for homemade Coke that you make at the house. Like artisanal pickles. Shit, you'd just go to jail.

Unless maybe you're white. Because in our society whites get away with more shit, but it's not like whites get away with everything, like you read on the internet. I mean, maybe the rich ones. Poor whites with tattoos and bad hair, the police fuck with them all the time. But it's probably still different. I mean, you can be a rich black and I bet cops still treat you like you just stole a pack of chewing gum. Poor blacks probably always get treated like they just stole a car.

And maybe that's why people don't get mad at the Bicycling Confederate circling the courthouse. Because if you get mad at him you have to be mad at so many things.

Or maybe I'm overthinking it.

I asked Bennet one time what he thought of him, and Bennet was like, "That dood's hysterical."

"Huh?"

"He's fucking crazy, man."

"He doesn't worry you? Like the flag."

"Nah, man. That corn-dick's on a bicycle."

That's what he called him. A corn-dick. We didn't have that term in Texas.

So, I was listening to the courthouse geese go honk, hoot, hutta and watching that corn-dick circle the square. Passing in front of the shops and restaurants. Disappearing behind the courthouse every so often. Reappearing in front of this restaurant called Broth that opened a few months before. I hadn't eaten there. It was the kind of restaurant my uncle called "faggy" but that really meant "nice."

It's always funny to me how if something seems like it's for rich people, overly straight men think it's "gay." At the same time, a man is more manly if he can pay for things. Like, how does that even work?

Brian Allen Carr

But as I sat there thinking about that, it occurred to me that maybe Broth was the type of place that would hire you for being able to cook an omelette, and I decided that the Bicycling Confederate wasn't going anywhere anytime soon, so I jumped off the bench and moseyed around to the back of Broth to kind of see if I could get a peek in the kitchen.

The alleys behind restaurants are some of the grossest places on earth. Gray water stands in slippery crags, and the bouquet of decaying food hangs like heat in the air. Bits of this and that lie scattered. Flies buzz and swirl. Cardboard rots in wet heaps. Steam heaves from the warmth of rotting, drags like poison mist in the cold air.

I hadn't been behind a ton of restaurants, but anytime I'd ever been behind a restaurant, I'd known it. Most businesses aren't like that. Most businesses can't be identified by their alleyways.

In fact, what other businesses can?

Anyhow, I stood there in the yuck of the alley watching the back door of Broth, and it was a screen door, and the kitchen was better lit than the decaf day, and I could see, every so often, cooks and dishwashers and waiters moving back and forth behind the screen, and you could tell that the lunch rush must've been over, because the waiters had their shirts untucked and the dishwashers were smiling and cussing.

And I was sort of drawn in closer toward that screen door, the way you accidentally move toward what you're paying attention to, and the closer I got the more I could smell herbs and oil and fire and soap, and I could hear all the hum and hiss and clank and clang.

And then there was a woman in the door holding a towel, and she dabbed at her nose with the back of a hand. "Need something?" she asked.

I said, "You think the chef would give me a job if I could make an omelette?"

She pushed open the screen door and I could see her face better and I could tell she was important. "I'm the chef. Women can be chefs, you know."

"Well would you?"

"Your people skills are shit," she said. She made to let go of the screen door, but I said, "Cooks gotta be good with people?"

She folded up her towel and draped it on the waist-rope of her apron. "No. But they can't be assholes. Not and work in my kitchen."

"I'm not an asshole though. My mom taught me to make omelettes, and my aunt told me that if I could make one well enough I could probably get a kitchen job."

"Well go home and tell your mom that she needs to teach you how to make an omelette and how not to be an asshole."

"She's dead."

"Ha," the chef said.

"Nine years in April."

"Then tell your daddy."

"He died eleven years ago in November."

"Bullshit."

"Kids can not have parents, you know."

She didn't soften at that, but you could tell she didn't hate me anymore. "I'm not looking for cooks."

"I changed my mind anyhow."

"Wait," she said, because I was about to walk away, to trudge through the grimy alleyway and go back to watching the Bicycling Confederate with the geese. "Come make me an omelette."

"What for? You're not hiring and I'm an asshole."

"Because I'm hungry and I don't feel like cooking."

It was the most logical thing I'd heard in forever.

Restaurant kitchens after a service look tragic. That's what Chef told me anyhow.

She said lots of things to me as she showed me around. It was like she gave me a tour before the omelette cooking even began. She wanted me to know where everything was, I guessed, but every time she showed me anything she told me about it too.

We moved in zigzags through the place. "Dish station," Chef said and pointed to the little man standing in front of the three sinks. He had a red do-rag on and smiled a wonky-tooth mouth at me. "Homer's what we call him, but just 'cause his last name's Simpson. What's your first name again?" You could tell it was a sort of joke they had.

"I keep forgetting," the dishwasher said. "It's tattooed on my dick if you wanna check."

Chef rolled her eyes. "Must be a one-letter name."

The dishwasher smiled. "That's it," he said. "It's DJ!"

"This way's the reach-in," Chef said, and we moved across this kind of orange and damp floor to a refrigerator with sliding doors, and she grabbed a black handle and tugged the door open on its tracks, and I was hit with the smell of a million springtimes. "All the herbs we have you'll find in here. Parsley. Thyme. Rosemary. Some chives. And green onion." As she named the herbs she pulled them forward so I could identify each and smell each individually in the catastrophe of their scents. So much odor, it felt like my brain did a belly flop. "We source most everything from Indiana. Michigan. Kentucky. When we can. This time of year though, these come up from Mexico."

"I'm from the border," I told her.

"Which one?"

"Texas-Mexico."

"Speak Spanish?"

"Not really."

She closed the reach-in. "We keep the eggs in the walk-in." She motioned for me to follow her to the back of the kitchen, and we went through a big metal door, passing through a curtain of slippery plastic. We stepped into a cold closet where we could see our breath, and again my mind went weird at all there was to sniff.

In my English class once, I had to learn the word *melopoeia*, which means when words are like music, so the language doesn't mean what it means, it means how it sounds.

You couldn't explain the smell of the walk-in with meaning, but you could get at it with melopoeia.

So: It was a raucous bundle of caramelized clutter and broke open iced death for sweet gagging funk plow. It was shiver fog berg odor. Rambunctious heaving raggle knuckles.

"The lady I get my eggs from tells me the names of her chickens, but I forget them all except for Ollie so I just call these Ollie's eggs." Chef showed me a few flats of eggs. She pointed to a shelf labeled DAIRY with big letters. "We have a few different cheeses," she said, but most of them I'd never heard of before. "We have a three-year cheddar from Fair Oaks Farms. We have unpasteurized Camembert. Parmesan."

"My omelettes are just eggs."

"Old-school," said Chef. "Grab some of Ollie's eggs then."

Chef led me to the line, and there was a huge vent hood over everything that huffed and buzzed, and the stovetop put off so much heat, I thought the meat on my arms would cook off.

"Ever been in a professional kitchen?"

My eyes bulged at the heat, but I couldn't really say anything.

"Hot as hell, huh?"

I kind of answered with my eyes.

Chef reached over to a rack above the line and plucked a non-stick pan from a hook. "This is MY egg pan. I usually don't let anyone use it but me. I won't cook eggs on anything but non-stick, but I know you're old-school." She smiled at me. "Would you rather cast iron?"

I took the pan from her. "Nah this'll do."

"What else you want?"

I looked around. "A bowl. A fork. A spatula. Salt. Pepper. Butter."

"Butter not oil?"

"Butter's better."

She rounded me up the things I needed, and y'all, I

killed that omelette. I broke my eggs, and forked them fluffy, and I spilled them into the pan at the perfect temp, and I made Ollie's eggs dance out that pan shaped like a football that was pale yellow as Sunday-school light, and Chef looked at my work and said, "Pretty impressive." The kitchen hissed. The smell of steam. The heat held everything still. Chef took a bite. "That's an omelette," she said.

"Well?"

"Well what?"

"Do I get the job?"

"I'm not hiring."

The kitchen seemed to tighten.

"You're skipping school, right?" Chef said. "You scared of what happened in Florida?"

"Florida?"

"The shooting?"

"Oh, shit, I forgot about that. Nah, I'm suspended."

"Oh," Chef said. The omelette just kind of set on the plate between us, and she sort of stood there with her fork in her hand, and then one of the waiters came up, and he had a ponytail.

"Front of house is good. I'm gonna run to the bank and," he paused and looked at me, tilted his head and squinted his eyes. "You look familiar."

"He's a suspended high school kid," Chef said. "So he probably shouldn't." She set her fork down.

"Well, hell, people see people in this town," said the waiter. And he was right. Every face in Opioid, Indiana, seemed familiar.

"I don't think I know you," I said.

He lifted a finger at me. "You're Joe Riggle's nephew. I met you at the apartment once. What's your name?"

"Riggle."

"Nah, your first name."

"First name is Riggle."

"Riggle Riggle?" said the waiter.

"Nah, Riggle Quick. My first name is my mom's last name. It's a thing we do back home. My momma and my uncle are brother and sister."

"Your dead mother?"

"Jesus, Chef," said the waiter.

"Well, they *were* brother and sister," I said.

"Shit," said Chef. "I thought you were fucking around. Your father too?"

"Yeah."

"What you doing back here?" the waiter asked me.

"Nothing," I said. "You seen my Uncle Joe?"

"Couple weeks ago. He drop off again? That boy's always falling off."

Chef threw away what was left of her eggs. "I got some stuff to do in the office. Will you show him out when you're done?"

"Sure," the waiter said.

"It's cool," I said. "I'm leaving. I'm done."

Chef held out her hand. "It was nice meeting you. Come back around. Maybe one of my cooks or dishwashers will get arrested or quit or OD or something. I'm sure I'll need somebody eventually. It's the nature of the industry. Pirates can't keep a ship beneath them too long."

"Okay," I said. Then to the waiter, "You got any idea where he drops off to?"

"Not really. I mean, I can call some people," he looked up at the clock, "but it'd be best to wait a few hours. You want my number? I doubt Peggy has it."

I dabbed at the sweat on my face, the heat from the kitchen just making me melt. "I guess."

He took a pen and a napkin from his pocket and wrote down a number that he gave me. "I used to run with your uncle more, but I quit that game. I'm too old. He knows he needs to settle down too, but knowing a thing and doing a thing are different things."

The waiter walked with me to the back door and told me to call or text that evening and he'd try to see what he could find out, and I stumbled back into the gray daylight and the sloppy alleyway, the sweat freezing on my skin, and I went back out to the square to see if the Bicycling Confederate was still there, and he was.

He had parked his bike and was sitting on a bench

surrounded by geese. I had built up nerve for talking to strangers, I'd figured. I mean, I'd cooked for a chef, which maybe isn't the biggest deal in the whole world, but it was one of the most important things I'd ever done. I'd had a few folks with verified accounts retweet me on Twitter and I met a Dallas Cowboys player whose name I couldn't remember and I'd gotten a hand job. But the omelette thing was, to me, a kind of big deal, and I guess I was living off that high a little bit, because I walked straight up to that Bicycling Confederate, touched his flag and said, "Why the fuck are you flying this?"

You ever talked to someone who you didn't think was medically stupid, and the split second after you say something to them you realize they might be?

You can't use the R-word. And I'm sure "medically stupid" isn't the most appropriate way to say it, but y'all, that Bicycling Confederate had a syndrome or was on the spectrum, I think. And I'm sure that's a horrible thing to say, but it also might explain a ton. He was holding a hot dog bun, tearing off bits that he flicked toward the courthouse geese, and they hissed and clucked toward him, pecking food off the ground. Their beady and vacant eyes glistened like glass.

"What you mean?" he asked me and flicked some bread. "I'm American. I got the right to do whatever I want." His mouth and his eyes seemed to be from two different people, like his face was cobbled together from bits of discarded faces, and there amongst the geese he seemed like some queer king of some bizarre empire.

"Bruh, that flag is *anti*-American."

"Libtard," he told me. "Snowflake." He spit toward the sidewalk, but he didn't get enough power behind it, and a trail of saliva slunk down his chin, and he wiped it away with his hot dog bun.

"Jesus," I said.

"Lord and savior." He tossed the spit-soaked bread at a goose who gobbled it gone.

Around that time, my phone shook in my pants, so I grabbed it out of my pocket and checked my texts. Bennet had hit me up on someone else's phone.

The text came through as a number and said this:

(317) xxx-xxxx: This bennet, they're talking about having the teachers carry

Me: Carry what

(317) xxx-xxxx: Guns hahahahahahahaahh

Me: What

(317) xxx-xxxx: At school to save us

Me: Id rather get shot

(317) xxx-xxxx: Hahahahahaha

"I got one of those things," the Bicycling Confederate said.

I pocketed my phone. "Sure you do."
Then he held his hand like this:

And he moved his hand close to the face of a goose and said, "He don't believe us," and he lowered and raised his thumb as he spoke so it looked like his hand was talking.

"What's with your hand?" I said, because what I saw was Remote.

"It's a goose, you idiot." He lifted his hand at me. "Honk, honk," his hand said.

My phone vibrated again:

> (317) xxx-xxxx: Who d'you think would be the worst teacher to have a gun.
> Me: I'm busy
> (317) xxx-xxxx: Then just don't text back

Me: What

(317) xxx-xxxx: Just don't text back if your busy it's
not that big a deal.

Then the Bicycling Confederate stood up, got on his
bike and screamed, "God bless America." He made
his hand like Remote one more time. "Honk, honk,
honk," he hollered, and he biked away, leaving me to
stand aloof in the congregation of geese who hooted and
bleated at me, I guess hoping I had bread.

My phone vibrated again, and I expected it to be
Bennet, but it was Peggy and she said this:

Peggy: Heard anything

Me: Nah, but i got a number

Peggy: Number?

Me: From a waiter guy. Texting him later.

Peggy: I'm at the apartment

Me: Okay

Peggy: You?

Me: On way home, i guess

Peggy: TTYL

On my walk home, I thought about what Bennet had
said and about all my teachers and which one I'd least

like to have a gun, but I think I came away with the idea that none of them should have guns anywhere let alone in school. I mean, can you imagine them telling you to be quiet if you knew they had a gun in their pocket. You know how awkward that would be? People are stupid as fuck.

The teacher would be like, "Sit down and be quiet or . . ."

"You'll shoot me?" some student would say.

And then the gauntlet would be thrown. I can't think of a more heroic way of dying than having a teacher shoot you rather than you sitting down and shutting the fuck up.

Hell, they'd have to name the hallway after you.

Peggy was about how you'd expect her to be. She was on the couch and was in pajamas, because she said that she had to get some rest. By pajamas, I mean a kind of tank top and some boxer shorts, and maybe I need to take a little while to explain what she looked like. This is one of those weird things, because if you're reading this, my guess is you don't want to hear me describe Peggy the way I want to describe her.

Listen, I'm a seventeen-year-old young man. I am a dick with a white boy attached to it. I'm serious. I've measured my penis when erect quite a few times, and on average it's average, and it drags me around half the time making me act like an asshole.

I get that this is viewed as a cop-out. That guys blame shit on their dicks or their hormones or how society raised them. And maybe it isn't just my dick. But it's my dick and the energy my dick has, and that energy is like a language that speaks to the rest of me in emotions, and those emotions are hard to say shut the fuck up to sometimes. And it's not always a creepy thing. It's just like peer pressure from inside you.

And so I was there in the room with Peggy. She's like maybe five foot four. And she has a tattoo on her right shoulder blade that says:

HOW TIME CAN MOVE

BOTH FAST AND SLOW

AMAZES ME

And she has mild, fascinating eyes. And her shoulders are smooth. And her body is well made. And basically whenever I'm around her I just want to look at her. And look at her. And look at her. I don't know.

"Get some rest," I said.

"I need someone to listen for my phone."

"I'll listen for it."

"But don't go playing on it."

"I won't."

Peggy wrapped herself up in a blanket on the sofa, and I went to my room and wondered about the Bicycling Confederate and Remote being on his hand. I know it wasn't Remote to him, but I still didn't want Remote on his hand. Remote was my mother's. Remote didn't belong to some racist Hoosier on a bicycle.

I got up and rummaged the kitchen for some dinner because I knew it didn't matter how the Bicycling Confederate held his hand, and I thought maybe I was just hangry, but nothing I ate seemed to take my hate away. So, I brooded around a bit before going back to bed.

Wednesday

On Wednesday I woke up worried. I'd had weird dreams that I can't do justice to describing with words.

I was trapped in these patterns that kept changing. I don't know if the patterns were like tunnels or mazes, or if they were more metaphorical than that. I mean, I saw them. And I saw me. But I don't know if I was inside patterns or if they were inside me or if it was somehow simultaneously a bit of both, but I kept seeing the patterns change as if I was trapped in a GIF, and each time I was about to figure out the logic behind the pattern the frame changed, and I'd go blind to the organization again, and my mind would sputter and hiccup, and then settle in as I learned the new formations, but then the pattern would morph again, and I never got free.

I sat up from sleeping, and I was sweaty like maybe

I had the flu. My mouth tasted like burnt carpet smells, and for about a minute I was lost—like I'd woken in the wrong body. The only other time I'd ever felt like that in Indiana was the first time I got blackout drunk, and I remember coming to in the weight room of some apartment complex, and there was a woman on a treadmill pretending not to notice me. I'd felt that a few times back in Texas. At least once at the group home and once at my father's father's and at my last guardian's.

This was different though, because I knew I should've known where I was. I mean, I knew all the stuff I saw in my room was mine, but I was fuzzy on how it came to be in its current location. My posters seemed to be on someone else's walls.

Then I settled into remembering, but I started worrying about my uncle.

I remembered I hadn't texted the waiter from the day before, so I found my phone and hit him up.

Waiting for texts can take forever, but I was still out of data, so I just turned on my flashlight and talked to Remote.

"Your week's been weird," he said.

"And it's not over," I told him. "Any clues as to what I should do?"

"I'm your hand, you idiot."

"Yeah but . . ."

"Anything Remote knows, you already know."

"Maybe."

"There's no maybe about it. My face is your fingers and your voice is my voice."

"But what about the other Remote? On the Bicycling Confederate's hand? Do you get to know what he knows too?"

"The only thing I know," said Remote, "is how Wednesday got its name."

Remote realized that the days established by the Graph of Kal the Ender could be used to solve problems. People could take each unit of time established

by the graph and spend those moments to focus on society's flaws.

But some of society's flaws could not be remedied with logic.

Insanity was one of those flaws.

Amongst all the insane Earthlings, one stood out as most astoundingly different. His name was Wed.

He would pull people's hair for no reason, and everything he drank he drank from a spoon as though eating soup, and he never decorated his home in observance of the seasons, and he didn't live in a regular house. He lived in a tree. He barely ever wore clothes. His hair was a tangled knot of dirt and twigs.

The only thing he was good at was catching things. He could catch rabbits and he could catch bears and if your children were sick, he could come and catch their colds or catch their pneumonia and he would take the sickness away with him to his tree and he would set the sickness free in his branches so his tree was always losing its leaves and getting better and growing them back again.

Earthlings discussed him with me often.

"Wed is a real problem, man," they said. "Sure he catches all the fevers, but I'm always finding him

naked in my yard eating water out of my well with a spoon. Something must be done."

At that time, little was known about the sun. We knew of the moon because of Mun and his infinite beard and we knew Kal the Ender was up there repeatedly killing him, but the sun was a great mystery, because no one could ever catch up to it to ask it questions. All we knew about it was it burned your skin if you stayed out in it too long.

"What if," I said, "we ask Wed to catch the sun for us? To ask it questions. To figure it out. He'll spend so much time naked in its rays it'll teach him a lesson, and he'll get dressed to avoid its burning him."

The Earthlings pondered this idea. On the one hand, they saw the logic in it and wanted Wed to wear clothes, but on the other hand, they worried. What if Wed could catch it? It was so danged hot. What if he was able to bring it home with him to his tree? Would we all catch fire?

Tues was there, and he offered this observation. "I have, when bored, fired several arrows at the sun, but I have yet to hit it. I doubt Wed is as fast as my arrows, but we could invite Wed to try to catch one before it falls. If he can, we rethink the endeavor. If he can't we offer him the task." Tues blew a great plume of smoke that shaped itself into Wed running and running and running after an arrow. "At the very least, he'll be gone from us forever."

So, Wed was invited to race an arrow.

Tues shot the fastest arrow he had, from the strongest bow he owned, and Wed darted out naked after it and disappeared into the distance.

The crowd that amassed to watch the race waited patiently for Wed to return from the distant horizon that he raced after.

He returned hours later with the arrow in his hand. "I caught it," he said.

The crowd was astonished, but Tues said, "As it flew?"

"The arrow never once rested," said Wed. "I can catch anything."

Tues noticed dirt in the feathers of the arrow, and he said, "Then we have another more difficult task for you."

"Just a moment," Remote said, because I was worried about the sun's heat.

But Tues took the arrow from Wed's hand and showed me the dirt. "It's okay," Tues said. "He can handle it."

"Oh," Remote approved. "If you say so." I looked out at the Earthlings. "I have faith in Tues."

"What's the task?" Wed asked.

"We want you," said Remote, "to catch the sun for us. If you think you can?"

Wed rubbed his head. "Do I get to keep the arrow?"

Tues handed it to him. "Why not?"

Taking the arrow from Tues, Wed turned the projectile, extended it in his hand and pointed it at the sun. "I've caught it," Wed said. "It will not move." He stood there sweaty, his naked body heaving and the arrow held above him.

The crowd gasped in shock.

"Are you sure?" I said.

Wed looked at the arrow. He looked at the sun. He looked back at Remote. "If you don't believe me just watch."

We did. We watched on and on. And, as we waited, the sun moved. So, too, did the arrow.

"Wed," said Tues. "The sun is moving and you are moving with it."

"No," said Wed. "I am being completely still. The direction of the arrow and the placement of the sun are unchanged."

At sunset, Tues challenged him again. "The sun is getting smaller," Tues said. "The horizon is eating it."

"It is doing no such thing. Watch on."

Tues sent for coffee. The Earthlings went home. Only insane people and Remote and warriors could endure such madness. Tues and I watched in the night as the arrow Wed held was finally lowered to the ground and aimed at his own feet. "Clearly you see now that the arrow is pointing at the Earth."

"It is pointing at the sun," Wed said. "The Earth is merely in its way."

At daybreak, Wed's arrow pointed to the exact spot at the exact moment where the sun crept into the sky.

"Alas," said Remote. "You have caught it! It hasn't moved from the arrow's line."

I made to relieve Wed of the arrow, to spell him from his task, to allow him to take his naked leave.

"Are you crazy?" said Wed. "It might escape if I lower the arrow."

For the rest of Remote's life, Wed stood there proudly nude, with his arrow pointed at the sun. In that way, Earthlings learned of time and watches, and we decided to name the middle of the work week after Wed, because he stayed centered on the sun.

When Remote showed him how the word Wedsday

was spelled, he grew appalled. "It's too plain," he said. "It needs something strange in the middle."

Remote added the letters NE to stand for Wed's never-ending task. WedNEsday.

I got a text back from the waiter that said he hadn't heard a peep, and I got out of bed and went to find Peggy. I wanted to see what she knew, but she wasn't around. And there wasn't a note. So, I sent her a text and took a shower.

I hadn't bathed for a while, and I wondered if maybe that was why my dreams were so weird. Like maybe dirt traps in bad energy. I always feel like, when I haven't bathed for a while, I get a kind of second skin of filth, and I considered to what extent that filmy layer might act like a sealant that keeps in negative thoughts.

Every time you ever see a picture of a killer on TV, they always look filthy, and maybe there's a kind of connection between being dirty and being violent, but of course my data was still gone, and I had no way of looking up anything.

I was having to make more decisions than usual, but they weren't decisions that affected anything, they were just kind of decisions about what to think. Like, I was in the shower shampooing my hair, and I had to come to terms with the idea that being dirty MIGHT have an impact on your likelihood of committing violent crimes, and just there being the two options made it certain that I had to decide which of the options was more likely to be true. I couldn't fact-check my own thoughts on my phone. I couldn't run anything by the internet. I had to just decide which thing was more likely ACCORDING TO ME.

And then it occurred to me that people used to never have phones. Could never do that. Where they looked everything up. They'd have to decide stuff just on whims.

So, I decided that being dirty made you more likely to be violent, but I knew good and goddamned well that there was a strong likelihood that when I finally got to google it, I'd be wrong.

Which means, if you think about it, that people probably used to be more comfortable being wrong. You'd think a thing and then a month would pass and you'd find out you were full of shit.

These days, you think a thing might be more likely, and then you look it up. You get to skip a step. The step where you choose and fail. Or choose and succeed. And that must have an effect on us. I don't know if it makes us stronger or weaker, or better or worse. But it makes us different than we used to be.

Also, since my data was gone, I got to just think up bullshit and be fine with it.

As an example: I was rubbing shampoo in my hair, and I was like: *Wonder what that name's from. Shampoo?*

But I knew there was no way I'd find out anytime soon, so I just thought up some bizarre bull crap to satisfy my curiosity. I decided that it was a mispronunciation of Sham's Poo, and there was a giant monster named Sham whose shit was somehow good for our hair, and he was captured and forced to poop into individual bottles, and that's what I was rubbing on my head. As I sudsed up, I envisioned poor Sham's life.

Here's how that looked:

Sham's Life

Sham was born on the third planet from Croptic 4, a white dwarf sun on the outer edges of the Tri-angulum Galaxy near the realm of Kloptuse. The planet was called Klaz 19. And all of Sham's kind were known as Shams.

Now, planets, like towns, have identities—things they're known for. Klaz 19 was known for scissors the way New Orleans is known for jazz. They made the best scissors in the universe. This is because their trees were made from a special steel that never dulled and also because they had lots of ugly diamonds that they used for their ax heads. Once upon a time Klaz 19 was made entirely of coal.

Brian Allen Carr

They'd use their ugly diamonds to cut their trees, and they'd use their trees to make the scissors, but on all of Klaz 19 there wasn't a single ribbon or sheet of paper or strand of hair. They had absolutely no idea what most beings used scissors for. They initially built scissors off a schematic they found on a wayward space broadcast that they'd intercepted with their satellite dishes, and prior to the scissors, no Sham had ever died.

They are biologically immortal, the Shams. Nothing kills them except for being cut by steel scissors.

It was quite fortunate they figured that out when they did, because Klaz 19 was getting overpopulated. They put to death all the riffraff with their scissors, and they started leading better lives, and so they considered the scissors holy, and they made them the way Christians make crucifixes and they wore them on chains.

When their planet was discovered by a mammalian life form, the scissors gained new purpose. Shams made and traded scissors for goods from other worlds.

Spices. Tobacco. Condoms. Fireworks.

But one day this one trader named Vidal came around and was a real dick. He showed up to trade bananas for scissors, and he called Sham their equivalent of the N-word. He called Sham a "dirty scissor."

Sham decided to teach him a lesson.

He shit in a water bottle and put it in Vidal's luggage, and on the way home Vidal found it and took a sniff. He asked his wife, "What do you think this is?"

And his wife took a whiff and was like, "Soap, you dummy."

She took a bath with it. Her hair had never shined brighter. They turned their spaceship around and went back to Klaz 19.

When Vidal got there, Sham was like, "Why are you back?"

And Vidal was like, "I need more of this." And he held up the bottle of Sham shit.

Sham laughed like a motherfucker, but his parents didn't think it was too funny. It was a great and terrible thing on Klaz 19 to give people Sham shit, on account of on Klaz 19 Sham shit was the worst smelling shit in the world.

They were super apologetic, the parents. They didn't want to offend Vidal: he was their best banana supplier, and bananas were Shams' favorite food.

"I might be able to overlook it," Vidal said, "so long as you give me your son."

Sham's parents were appalled. "We can't give you our son."

Vidal was adamant. "No son, no more bananas."

They didn't have to think long. "Nice knowing you, son," the father said.

And Sham was tied up and put in a cage on Vidal's spaceship, and that's where he still lives to this day.

Even right now, Vidal is feeding Sham bananas, and Vidal's wife is catching Sham's Poo inside plastic bottles to be sold at the store.

When I got out of the shower, I had a text from Bennet from a number I didn't recognize.

(317) xxx-xxxx: Miss me yet?
Me: Don't you ever pay attention in class?
(317) xxx-xxxx: I'm multitasking.

Then I heard the front door, and I went out into the living room in my towel.

"Why aren't you out looking for your uncle?" Peggy asked me. She was jittery but beautiful, and I was in my towel and I thought about letting it drop from my body, but I thought that would be very bad. Like assault or something.

"I'll go," I said.

"He's not usually gone this long with no word."

"Should we call someone?"

"Who? The cops? And tell them what? That we're missing our druggie?"

"I mean . . ."

"I've already tried everyone he knows. I'm getting a bunch of nothing."

"Then what's me looking for him going to do?"

"It has to beat nothing."

"Drive me around. We'll look together."

"I have to go up to Indy."

"Why?"

"To check up there. I mean, there are some places he goes I can't take you."

I knew that. There were trap houses and all. Dive bars. Rotten places. Homes where children dawdled in filthy diapers as mothers played app games on cracked phone screens. Rank abodes with rotting carpet. Abandoned corners. Swollen neglect.

I'd been in places like that. Where TVs babysat

children. Where soup bowls sat crusty on sofa cushions. The taste of recent smoking lingered. A fight could break out whenever.

Before my parents died, those were figments, man. And I guess I get a bit in shock at just the words "trap house," because the first place I went to, when the courts were deciding where to place me, was some group home for kids like me, though calling them "like me" is like saying we were mammals.

I started reading this book one time that said, "Happy families are all alike; every unhappy family is unhappy in its own way." Maybe that's right. I think about it all the time. The book was too long and I didn't finish it, so maybe the author changed his mind by the end.

But as far as I can tell happy families operate like this: they love each other and do their things. Unhappy families can look all kinds of different. Kids can be orphans or mothers can be crack addicts. Children can be R-word. Fathers can be secret gay. Each little broken part of people looks different.

I was in a home with eight other kids once and some of them had mothers in jail and some of them had never seen their fathers. Was their unhappiness like mine?

If my mom was locked up, but I knew I'd see her again, would I feel the same kind of sad as the sadness of having one morning jumped up on her bed and pulled back her blankets to see her frozen still in death. Her mouth opened and tight. Her eyes wide at the sky.

If my mom was in jail, would I have stood on the front lawn that morning in my underwear waiting for a neighbor to wonder what I was doing and call the police?

If I'd never seen my father, never met him, would I think about his truck? How he fell asleep at the wheel and drifted off the road and how they'd found his semi burning and how his charred body was identified by his teeth?

If you're happy because your mother and father are happy and alive it looks the same whether or not they are dentists or ballerinas, whether or not they are pimps or policemen. Only difference is you might eat dinner at different restaurants, but you'd still eat dinner together. You'd sit across the table and talk about your days.

"What was the best thing about your day?" your father might ask.

"I got an A on my math test."

"And the worst thing?"

You'd stare off at bullshit. "My tummy ached during second period."

For me? No one's asking, so I can't say:

Best thing: no one I know died.

Worst thing: my junkie uncle is missing.

And when I was at that house, the whole place grimy

and the other orphans moaning and shitting themselves, some so disfigured their arms and legs were shaped like boomerangs and they wore bibs to catch drool, my unhappiness was different then.

I was nine. I thought I'd gone to hell.

I got dressed and was walking up and down the streets of Opioid, Indiana, with really no goddamned aim in mind and no goddamned clue.

How do you even begin to look for a druggie?

They operate under different gravities, are fueled by different suns. They wake with a time no one else moves to.

I've seen my uncle so bent he can't stand out of his chair, and he'll think he should drive. The reason for that is, when he's wasted, he likes to be in his car.

"It's the only place you can control everything," he told me once. "You can diddle the radio and change the temperature, and you can even decide where to be. Don't like the vibe of a place, you just drive somewhere else." I saw his face through a three-day beard when he told me this, and the hairs on his chin were going white, and his eyes looked aimed at something far away. He seemed like he could hurt a baby. "Bump duh bum," he said, and smiled at me. "You're judging me with your eyes."

But his car had been in its space in the parking lot earlier, and I had watched Peggy climb into it to drive up to Indy to see if she could scratch him up, and it was 21 degrees outside but she had told me to stay out looking for at least a few hours, to ask anyone I saw walking around if they'd seen him.

"Junkies know junkies, and junkies are always on foot."

"Yeah, but . . ."

"It's getting to be like that," she told me. "No one's seen him, and there's really no one to call. If we call the cops, what will they do with you?"

I hadn't thought of that. I wouldn't be a minor much longer, but until then I had to be somewhere, and I didn't want to go back to a group home. The last one was full of ants that climbed on the walls. Everything about group homes is creepy-crawly.

"I'll look," I promised Peggy. "I'll look everywhere."

And there I was on foot moving in whatever direction I was aimed in as though the streets of Opioid, Indiana, would somehow cough up my uncle from the concrete and he'd lie there on the sidewalk gasping for breath and coming to, look up to me after a minute lost in a junkie jag and have me drag him home.

It's weird combing the streets for stray junkies.

The day was a filthy gray cat rubbing its ribs on the asphalt. Purring its coldness. Whipping its tail.

I couldn't stream shit for music, and I only had two albums on my phone. One was a Wu-Tang album, but it was just instrumentals.

For about three months back in Texas I had tried to be a rapper, but then Erika told me I couldn't.

"That's not okay," she told me.

I'd used this Wu-Tang song called "Think Differently" for my beat, because you couldn't use a beat everyone knew, and Wu-Tang was just old enough to be forgotten but just new enough to sound good, and I'd written these bars:

> I'm the world's deadliest orphan
> And you cannot get rid of me
> Pack me up and ship me off
> And call my breaths felonies
> I am not a broken pencil
> My sharp end's for sentences
> Mess it up and turn around
> and rub to get rid of it

"Aye, no," said Erika.

"What?"

"It's no good. You're too white."

And my rap career was over.

But I was listening to Wu-Tang instrumentals and

walking up and down the streets thinking, since the day was a gray cat: *here*, *junkie*, *junkie*, *junkie*.

I was looking in parked cars and under parked cars. I dunno, I was looking everywhere.

Now, remember when I told you that I am always finding the last thing I was looking for? Well sometimes I find things I forgot I was looking for at all.

I was on some street, hell I can't even remember now, and I was carving my eyes this way and that, and I heard a kind of "hoo hoo," but it wasn't an owl.

It was Autistic Ross, propped up on a retaining wall in front of some yard, smiling and licking his teeth and batting his eyes. He had his hands together and he was rubbing them. He was wearing overalls tucked into rubber boots. An unzipped windbreaker, and a shirt that said JESUS SAVES on the chest. He looked like a candy farmer. Like, if there existed a world where candy was farmed, where farmers went out into the dirt and yanked up lollipops, that's what Autistic Ross would be.

"Autistic Ross," I said to him.

And he said, "Ho, ho, hello." And he smiled and his cheeks blushed joyfully. Some people just like what they are. When people are like that, they're always happy to see other people. "Young man," he said. "Young man." His voice sounded like he had a bubble in his throat or like his saliva was sour.

I had talked to him once or twice in some place I couldn't remember, about a friend he used to have. A baseball player. And I asked, "Do you remember me?"

"Not at all," he said. He squinted. "Should I? Are you going to try to sell me a car?"

"Oh, I don't . . ."

"We family?"

"No."

"I got family all over and I never really learned to drive," he said. "I got a cousin in Alaska. I've only talked to him once. On the phone. I asked how's Alaska, and he said it was cold. But it's cold here," he said, "so maybe that's not far. Is Alaska far?"

"Yes," I said, "it's far."

"That's what I thought," he said. "It sounds far. Like the moon." He laughed. "Like the dadgum moon."

"Dadgum," I said, because I was jealous of how he said it. I wanted to feel the word in my mouth. But I don't think it felt for me the way it did for him. For him, it looked like he felt sweetly guilty for saying it. Like when you're five and you say the word *vagina* to your mom.

"I don't got family on the moon though," he said. He winked. "That I know of." Ross started looking at his hands. Like he was hoping that in them there was some clue to what he should talk about next, and there was a weird quiet moment, so I figured I'd ask about my uncle.

"I don't guess you know Joe Riggle?"

"Joe?" said Ross. His mouth wrestled around on his face, and his gaze drifted this way and that. "Not one iota."

"Iota," I repeated.

"Not a drop or a dime. But I'm working on something really great."

"What's that?" I said, and I expected to hear some dirty secret. Like Autistic Ross knew a place to watch some pretty teen through a window get naked before showering, or where you could stand and listen to people fucking on an evening.

"Look at this," he said. And he held up his hand like this:

I backed up. "Why you doing that?"

"It's a game," Autistic Ross said.

"A game?"

"For a game."

The whole world seemed to shift. Go crooked. Things were becoming things they never were, and I didn't know if I'd ever felt that way. Like all of Opioid, Indiana, was shrieking to a close, and I started thinking my mom was near me. Like I could smell her or feel her breath or something, and the next thing I knew, I was jogging away from Autistic Ross with this vague notion that I was being watched or manipulated or cared for. I couldn't quite tell. There was a presence and it had intentions, but I couldn't explain it. I buried my hands in my pockets, curious at the enormity of it all.

I got a text from a number I didn't know, and it said, "Still want a job?"

"Maybe," I texted. "Who's asking?"

"Chef," the text said. "At Broth. In?"

I needed something to take my mind off Autistic Ross's hand. "Sure?"

"Call," Chef texted me.

So, I did.

"Here's the deal," Chef said over the phone. "It's not

cooking. Yet." There was all kinds of commotion going on behind her. Voices and banging. The sound of water running or simmering food. "My dishwasher has to take a day for family stuff and I need someone to cover Friday night. I thought tonight you'd come in and learn. You'll get paid, and I'll feed you. Friday night you'll come in for real. You in?"

I didn't want to wash dishes, but I wanted to do something. So, I told her I'd be there. I had nowhere else to go. I moved along the streets hoping to chance into junkies and trying not to think about Remote.

Chef was behind Broth having a cigarette, leaned against a wall, the greasy alleyway glimmering around her. She had tattoos on her arms. On her right forearm there was a knife perched in flowers. On her left forearm there was a band of pans rimmed with fire. Her arms rested at her sides. Her right leg was bent so her clog rested against the brick wall of Broth. Her cigarette dangled from her lips. She plucked it free when she saw me. "There he is," she said. "Lil Tex. Can I call you that? I call everyone something, and you kids are all something. Lil Peep. Lil Pump. Or you could be Omelette." She took a drag and blew smoke. "Don't get into these," she said, kind of holding the cigarette at me. "They're impossible to kick."

"You should try vaping," I told her.

"I have. It sucked." She dropped her cigarette, stomped it out, emptied her lungs and drew a deep breath of the alley-scented air. She blew breath and it steamed away from her face. "You can't tell when you're done smoking in the winter," she said, and she motioned me to follow her.

When we went into Broth this time, it was different. Before I felt like an intruder. This time I felt like a guest. Everyone I saw smiled at me, like they knew I was coming, and it felt good. I don't know. I'm not sure the last time I'd felt that way. I was new, but I was approved, I guess.

"You like tacos, right?" Chef said. "Jorge is from Puebla," she motioned to a line cook with a shaved head and a chin piercing. "He makes tortillas in-house. He's doing mollejas for family meal. Ever had that?"

"Mollejas or family meal?"

"Mollejas."

"Yeah. Cow glands are banging."

"Fuckin' A," said Chef.

Jorge liked that I was from the border, and he wanted me to be served first, and he insisted we eat before anything else happened. We carried plates and pans into the dining room where the empty room sat in anticipation of that night's service. I had never been in a restaurant that closed between lunch and dinner, so one of the waiters explained it to me when he saw I looked confused.

"Split service," he said to me. "We do lunch. We close. We clean. We do dinner. We get off our feet in between. Eat. I have a glass of wine. Chef has two beers."

"Three beers," said Chef. She winked at me.

We sat at a long table that had been stripped of service items. That's what I learned to call them, "service items." Someone passed around a basket of tortillas that Jorge made, and then rice. Then beans. Finally mollejas. I twisted up a taco while Jorge talked to me.

"I don't fuck around," he said. "I poach them in brine. I take them out. Clean them. I grill them over oak. Then I marinate them in adobo. Then I sauté to finish."

They were insane good. Smokey and crunchy. "Best I've had," I said.

Conversation clucked around. Who had done what over the past few days. Who had been laid. Who had been drunk. Chef said, "I wanna get some mushrooms and hike when it warms up. Go down to Brown County, hang with the hippies and trip out. Ever been?" she asked me. She swigged her Pacífico.

"Tripping?"

She about choked on her beer. "To Brown County?" she said.

I had not.

After we ate, we piled back into the kitchen, and I worked with Homer to get ready for the night. I had washed plenty of dishes at home, but this was an entirely different ordeal. It was industrial. It was hardcore. There were three sinks and a dishwasher that kind of worked like a conveyor belt.

Small stuff, stuff that went into the dishwasher, would be rinsed off in the center sink and then set on a tray that looked like a wide and short milk crate. The tray was then pushed into what looked like an elevator shaft. Then you'd pull a lever, and the shaft would close and a cycle would run for about two minutes. You'd lift the handle and slide the dishes out and they'd be piping hot and the air would taste like soap and steam.

With larger dishes, it went like this: you'd set them in the center sink and spray them off. You'd be spraying hunks of chicken and scraps of vegetables. All that would accumulate into a drain that you'd have to fish clean with your hands every so often—grabbing fists full of chewed food, your hand held like a claw.

Once the big shit was off, you'd plunk the dishes

down into the hottest water bath you could fathom in the far left-hand sink. In there, you'd submerge the pans or whatever, and you'd scrub like hell with this thing that looked like steel dreadlocks. The textures were unnerving. The soap scum would bubble and pop. The water would get murky and glisten with grease. Your hands, invisible in the murky dishwasher, falling apart as the steel scragged the pan surfaces.

When the dish was clean, or as clean as you could get it because it was like some burnt stuff just wouldn't come off, you'd rinse it again and set it in the far-right sink that was filled with cool bleach water. Then you'd pull it out, towel it off, and put it away so it could just get dirty again.

But the first thing I had to do, even before all that, was I had to put on an apron. Now, it's weird, because I had never worn an apron before, but I had seen my mother wear an apron, and her apron and this apron weren't the same kind of apron. I don't know. Hers was dainty. This thing was like putting on a pair of Dickies or work boots.

It was black with purple string to tie it around my belly, and I slid it over my neck and wrapped the ties around me twice and did a shoestring knot in front of me, and I don't know, I felt good in it. Clean or proud. And then the phone was ringing and I was listening to Homer and Homer was showing me how to test the pH of the bleach water. And then Chef came to me in the prickly light of the kitchen with her mouth clenched in a kind of fake frown. "Good news and bad," she said. "Maybe. I got a fuck ton of tables," she said. It was so weird to hear her cuss. On the one hand, she seemed like she shouldn't. She was this little woman with angular features and eyes green like plastic. On the other hand, her voice seemed to hold cuss words the way seashells hold the sound of oceans. "You wanna stay on the whole night? I'll pay you off the books. Cash. Ten an hour. We need the help."

I wiped my hands on my apron. "Sure. I ain't got shit else to do," I said.

She put her hand on my shoulder. "You're in my kitchen," she said. "I demand respect. You call me Chef." Her gaze drilled through my eyes. "So: I ain't got shit else to do, Chef," she told me.

"I ain't got shit else to do, Chef," I said.

The shift came at me fierce. There was water and food and noise and steam. There was the constant hooting and hollering of the cooks, the constant chirping of the waiters. The click, clack plang of things being chucked, scuttled and lobbed. Hell-hot pans shrieked as they hit the water. The perfume of grease sat in my throat like cheese.

Chef stood in a service window calling for food. She

set up the plates and then she called out for servers. "Table twenty-seven up for service. Fire two chops. Both mid-rare. I need a side of frites. I need two orders of roast suck." I guess she felt my eyes on her. "That's succotash, Lil Tex," she hollered at me. "I'll teach you tons if you're around long enough."

My main thing was I ran back and forth from the dish station carrying bus tubs of dirty dishes and ferreting back clean stuff to where it went. Homer said that would be best, because I'd learn where everything went, but I'd get lost in the returning of things, and I stood looking back and forth to figure out where stuff went.

"You stoned?" said Chef.

"Hell no."

"Hell no, Chef," she barked.

She pointed out where I was headed to and I'd refocus with purpose. "Yes, Chef."

There was a music to the disorder, a dance to the melee. I had to change my apron twice on account of getting so wet, and even then my pants got soaked bad enough that when I went to take a piss my dick had pruned like it was a finger and I'd been swimming all summer.

But as busy and crazy as service was, the end of the shift was when the real hell hit. The kitchen closed down, and holy fuck it was like the cooks assaulted us with every dish ever made. Vast heaps of hotel pans and sheet trays were stacked at our feet and at one point Homer and I looked up from a deep stew of dirty dishes and dishwater with something like horror in our eyes, but Homer said, "They picked the wrong fuckers to fuck with," and made a face like a pirate might. His teeth looked like yellow stones. And we were strugglers together doing the dance of a million dishwashers before us, drenching our bodies and busting our fingers. Puckering our hands out and grinding away at the filth.

And you know what?

It took forever, but we peeled and pried and produced. We mashed our hands in and out of hot water, scraped away bits of pork caramelized to stainless steel. Shredded burnt cream from saucepans. Rinsed bubbles off everything. And everything. And more.

We were animals of water and soap. Emperors of spray nozzles. Masters of disasters. Scrubbers of the scum. And we got it all clean except a single cutting board and a pot.

"We always leave a little something for the morning," Homer told me. "Dish fairies."

After the shift, Chef paid me eighty dollars in mostly ones. "Titty tickets," she said, and the waiter who knew my uncle gave me a ride home, and he was a talker. We were only about a mile away but he ran his mouth the whole time we drove. He seemed normal at first. He knew my uncle, and he got me the job, and he drove a Toyota that was clean as a new penny inside though it smelled of old smoke, and he listened to Rolling Stones and he smelled like a regular person.

But as soon as we started moving, he started asking me about school. "There a lot of kids with troubles these days?" he asked.

"Troubles?"

"Well," he said, and he messed with his ponytail, "when I was your age we said *retarded* but my guess is you kids never use that word."

"Some people call it the R-word," I told him. "Teachers call those kids challenged. Or handicapped."

"Yeah, we had different words for it too. *Delayed* was one. *Special*."

"I was in a group once and the head lady called it blessed. But that was just like *her* word."

"Well they're as blessed as any, I guess. If any of us are. But there's more these days than there used to be."

"More?"

"More blessed," he said. "More challenged."

"Maybe."

"No, it's true. Not that it's anything against your generation." He drummed his fingers on the steering wheel.

"It's for a reason there's more of them, but you wouldn't believe me if I told you."

I assumed he was right, so I just kind of sat there quietly, and the blue glow from the clock light twinkled on my dish-soap polished fingernails.

"Ain't curious?" he asked me.

I moved an air vent. "Sure," I told him.

"It's on account of artificial intelligence," he told me. "AI."

"You think they're androids or something?"

"You know AI?"

"I'm seventeen and I've never had sex. I know AI."

"*They* aren't AI," he said. "They're being *used* for AI. We don't know how the human brain works. You see?"

I most certainly did not.

"And that term: AI. Artificial intelligence. What does that even mean?"

"Mean?" I said.

"Like the meaning of the phrase. Just at face value."

"Intelligence," I said. "That's artificial," I told him.

"Okay, so let's say you've got an artificial diamond. What's that artificially trying to be?"

"A diamond."

"But if we don't know how a human mind works, how can we even begin to understand how to create artificial intelligence? It'd be like trying to make an artificial diamond without knowing what a real diamond was. Do you know what a diamond is?"

"Of course."

"Could you make me one?"

"'Course not?"

"So how is a computer supposed to create fake intelligence if the people who designed the computer can't even tell a computer what intelligence is? Intelligence isn't the right word, and I think it matters what you call something. Like, we almost called this town Schortville."

"We might've been Schorties."

"Exactly," he said. "What you call a thing changes so many things."

"And this has what to do with the blessed kids?"

"Well, we can't know how the human mind works until we measure it against a similar but different mind. That's why there's so many autistic kids these days and stuff. The government *blessed* them so we could measure their minds against our own, and that reveals clues about our own intellects. It's like A/B testing. They are the controls in some experiment to help us be able to tell computers how the mind works so we can get true AI someday. Then people like you and me won't matter anymore at all. Who needs a meat machine like you or me when you can build robots that do what we do better and never need to sleep?"

"I guess."

The waiter fumbled a cigarette from beneath the dash of his car, put it in his mouth and lit it. "Schorties," he said. "I like that."

"Me too."

"Got me thinking," he said. "You try out on Schort Way? Looking for your uncle?"

"Where?"

"There's some houses out there."

But the waiter did something weird then. He took the cigarette out of his mouth, but he held it like this:

"Your uncle used to hang out some on Schort Way."

I stared at the cigarette. Smoke slipped from its cherry. "Do you always hold your cigarettes like that?"

"Weird as fuck right?" He smiled and smoke poured from between his teeth. "Can't seem not to. My friends ask me why I don't just stop, but if I was good at quitting things, I'd just quit smoking. That's the other thing about robots," he said. "They do what they're supposed to and they don't smoke or do drugs."

We pulled up to my apartment complex and the waiter parked. "Good luck," he told me.

I walked inside and Peggy was cross-legged on the sofa, her face draped toward her crotch. But she snapped up as soon as I stepped inside and popped to her feet and said, "Where the hell you been?"

"Working," I told her.

"Working?"

"Doing things for people in exchange for money."

"Don't be a smart-ass. When did you get a job?"

"Today," I said. "It was like a trial. Washing dishes."

Peggy sat back down and scrolled through her phone. She whispered to herself. She sort of shook her head. "Tomorrow's Thursday," she said.

"I know."

"Day after's Friday."

"That's how it works."

"Were you like this to your mother?"

I couldn't remember. I didn't think so. "Dunno."

"Well Friday is rent due. It's just about a week your uncle's been gone. Those two things don't worry you?"

"I got a job didn't I?"

"They gonna pay you eight hundred dollars before Friday?"

"You working? You making money? You doing shit?"

She held up her phone. "I'm looking for your uncle."

"Call the cops or something."

"Think the cops would upgrade you from here? Take you off to some nicer place?"

I thought again about the group homes. "Tomorrow," I said. "I'll look all day."

I showered that night, but I didn't use shampoo. Man, it's weird, but I got a guilty feeling when I reached for the bottle, and it was all on account of that bullshit story I told myself, but I guess I was so beat that I didn't want to contribute any more to Sham's imaginary suffering, and I got this flash of an idea that if I only didn't use shampoo every so often, the need for shampoo would diminish and maybe Sham would somehow, someday, get to go free.

I was only sort of clean when I climbed into bed, and I still didn't have any data, so I shined a light on the back of my hand and there Remote was staring at me with his one giant eye, and I kept thinking about the Bicycling Confederate and Autistic Ross and the waiter, and how Remote had been on their hands. I'd never seen him before anywhere except with my mom, and now he seemed to be everywhere I turned in Opioid, Indiana. I couldn't figure it out. I turned off my flashlight, plugged in my phone and went to sleep.

Thursday

I slept hard as hell. I'd never worked like that before. I'd done homework and I'd done lawn work, and I'd had my job sacking groceries, but I'd never done the kind of work that kicked your ass and you got paid for. It was a different kind of feeling. It was claustrophobic.

Running dishes for Homer, scrubbing pots with him, was painful, but I felt like I couldn't leave if I wanted to. I was stuck there doing what I was doing. It's the same when you're at school. When you're in your desk. When the teachers are going on and on. But it's different with school because you don't want to be there at all, so you just sort of zone out. Go into max-chill mode. Dick with your phone or doodle on paper or look off at other kids and wonder what they had for breakfast. Their mouths hung open. Their faraway eyes. But at Broth, part of me wanted to leave, but something in me also made me want to stay. It was hard work, but I was making money. And if Chef had come up and said, "Leave," it would've broke my heart some. Even though washing dishes was a pain in the ass. Being at school's not nearly as brutal, but when my principal suspended me, I was a happy-ass struggler.

There's this weird internal tension in working. Like when you touch the north poles of two magnets together and feel that push. It's a good push. But it eats energy. Because to get done what you want to get done—touching the same poles, getting your work finished—it takes something out of you. I slept and had heavy and dirty dreams of work and steam and dishwater. I floated on bubble-capped seas of brown liquid with bits of food bobbing here and there, and I clung to a hunk of bread to keep me afloat in the vast ocean of dishwater. I smelled the stink of slurping drains, the warmth of heaving garbage. And I woke in a way I never had. My eyes crept open and the room was silent and my skeleton felt clean, and my meat felt filthy. My muscles. My tendons. I dunno. They felt gross. But somewhere deep inside, I felt new.

I woke to text messages. Bennet was hitting me up and telling me about school. He said the kids were taking a vote to see who would be the best teacher and worst teacher to have a gun. Also, they were voting to see who was most likely to come to school and shoot the place up.

He was on some new number.

(317) xxx-xxxx: Who you got, man? We're taking bets.

Me: Huh?

(317) xxx-xxxx: Most likely to shoot up the school?

Me: I dunno. What's everyone else saying?

(317) xxx-xxxx: I think that kid Shelby Frank. Fuckers always got angry fists.

Me: He ain't that bad.

(317) xxx-xxxx: Who then?

I thought about it. It's an odd thing to consider. Who might break? Who might go home one day and decide they'd had enough of something? Who would curl up to violence like that? Like a blanket to protect yourself from the cold of the world with. Because violence is warm. Have you ever gotten angry? So angry you could hurt a thing? Your body feels like fire. And maybe that's what those kids are looking for. That feeling. Because it's so strong, it must be there for a reason.

I don't think I believe in God entirely, but I believe in something. I believe that we exist for something. That things happen for reasons. That our paths follow something like orbits.

My parents never really told me what they believed. My mother took me to church a few times after my father died, but we didn't go enough to learn people's names.

My father's funeral was a small thing. A few of his family members. We went to a golf course in a community where his oldest brother lived and we sat in a clubhouse with so many windows it felt like an aquarium. A player piano played hymns and there were about a dozen of us, and people sat in a circle telling stories about my father, and there was a picture of him on an easel. Most of the folks there were relatives, but there was a trucker or two who knew him from work, and they sat quiet with their faces aimed at the carpet, and I don't know that anyone ever mentioned God.

But I remember my mom after Dad died, and I remember she had two modes. She was either staring off at nothing and holding her face, or she was slamming things around and cussing under her breath. And one time I told her that she was always angry, and she said that if she wasn't supposed to be angry she wouldn't be angry.

"When you're thirsty it's because your body needs a drink," she told me. "When you're angry it's because your body needs something else."

"What?" I asked her.

"You heard what I said."

"What does your body need? When you're angry."

She scooped me up and held me to her. "Who knows?"

I think she was right. Sometimes you feel so terrible that all you know is that you need something, and when people feel that way, they go out looking. My uncle went out looking for drugs. My mother went out and found death. I think those shooter kids go out looking for violence. They think it will stop the ache they have, but my guess is it doesn't. I wanted to google it. I wanted to search up how school shooters felt afterward. Did it help them? Did it give them purpose? Did they get to jail and feel free from the pain, or did it just give them new pain to deal with? Or if they die there in a shootout or by turning the gun on themselves, do they get something like closure? A final bit of peace? A miraculous answer from God?

I think, if you asked an adult, they'd say it just gives them more pain, but that's probably not true. It probably gives them *different* pain.

I feel like there are two types of misery in this world. There's not getting what you want and being angry. And there's getting what you want and being sad.

If you're either one of those—if you're miserable—you don't know what will fix it. You go back and forth forever. Wanting a thing. Pursuing a thing. Getting a thing. Not wanting it. And you start all over again.

So the question wasn't who would shoot up the school. The question was: who might think shooting up a school would make them feel better than they feel right now.

And I didn't know how to answer that.

Me: Fuck if I know.

(317) xxx-xxxx: Fine. What's your porn name then.

We're also doing porn names.

Me: Porn names?

(317) xxx-xxxx: It's your first pet's name. And the name of the street you grew up on.

I had never really had a pet, but in my fourth-grade class we hatched chicken eggs in an incubator, and each of the students was responsible for a chicken for a short time, and my chicken was named McCluck. He was a Rhode Island Red, and when they are chicks they are black like crows, and I remembered watching him climb out of his brown shell and slump gross and slimy onto a Styrofoam plate, heaving breath and exhausted. The street I grew up on was Forester Way.

Me: McCluck Forester Way?

(317) xxx-xxxx: You had a dog named McCluck? You can leave off the way part.

Me: A chicken.

(317) xxx-xxxx: McCluck Forester is a pretty good porn name.

I didn't know if it was or not, but I sat thinking about my life on Forester Way, and my time with McCluck the chicken, but then it occurred to me that the apartment was quiet as fuck. So I bounced out of bed and scraped around the place, calling out "Peggy," but no one was there. I was hungry, so I made four toaster waffles and brewed some coffee. I'm not very good at brewing coffee. I've watched it done plenty, and I follow all the right steps, but every time I make it, it tastes funny. Too weak or too strong, but maybe it's just something that's better when someone else makes it. Like sandwiches or jokes. Like, when you tell yourself a joke, it's never as good as when someone else tells it to you. I could listen to jokes I know all day so long as they're coming out of someone else's mouth, but when they come out of my mouth, they never seem new.

That was one of the great things about Remote. He could tell me things that I already knew and they'd be funny again.

Here's how Remote told me Thursday got its name:

There came a disease called thirst that could only be cured with rain. Before that, we never felt compelled to drink anything. After thirst, we'd check the skies hoping for clouds.

"Do you think it will rain today?" we'd ask each other. If it didn't, our tongues would go dry and we'd have a hard time swallowing. Our heads would ache. Our muscles would cramp. It was god-awful.

We went to Wed to see if he could catch the disease and release it in his tree, but he was busy keeping the sun where it was with his arrow, his gross penis hanging nude between his legs.

"What will we do, then?" Remote asked aloud to no one in particular.

"Just drink rain when you can and deal with it," said Wed.

Our knowledge of weather wasn't fully formed so Remote said, "Well, can you move the sun back a ways? Whenever it rains, it seems like the sun is farther away. And we are terribly thirsty."

"It's not farther away," said Wed. "The sun just goes behind clouds. In the hills there is a woman named Jupiter who can tame clouds. Go to her."

Remote did. I journeyed into the mountains and found Jupiter sitting on a throne of mist. She had beautiful legs that had never been shaved and breasts covered by long black hair. Other than that she was naked.

"We are plagued by a new disease," Remote said in a raspy, thirsty voice.

"It is not a new disease," said Jupiter. "It's an old disease that you only just realized you've always had. You've grown into it the way young people grow into wanting sex."

"Either way," Remote said. "What do we do? We need rain. We heard you can tame clouds. Can you make it rain more for us?"

Jupiter made it lightning. She made it thunder. "There are other people in this world and they need the rain too. I can tame the clouds, I can't make more of them."

Remote was not happy at all. If I was less thirsty, I would have cried tears.

"Also," said Jupiter, "think about how much better the rain tastes after you've been thirsty a while. Think about how grateful you'll be when it finally does rain."

Remote tried a final plea. "Help us and we'll name a day after you."

"I don't want anything named after me. I want to be remembered the way lightning is remembered: as thunder. The way rain is remembered:

as puddles. I want to leave an impression, not a memory."

"What if," Remote said, "you just make it rain for us once. Just one hard rain. That way we can all cure our thirsts one last time. And after that, it will just be a thing we have to live with. But we will remember you always for the thirst that you took from us, and we will call your day Thirstday and it will be your impression upon us?"

Jupiter leaned back into her throne of mist. "I like it," she said.

With a flick of her wrist, she sent all the clouds on Earth to the place where Remote lived, and a great storm broke out, and Remote and the Earthlings all drank deeply of Jupiter's rain.

But it kept coming down. And coming down. It was more rain than we'd ever seen. It was way more rain than we'd ever hoped for. It was too much rain. The streets washed away from us. Anything not fixed to the Earth was lost to the flood. We sought refuge inside.

I was in bed with my phone, thinking about being McCluck Forester, and then I remembered what the waiter had said about the houses on Schort Way.

I texted the last number that had hit my phone, and I said:

Me: Look up a street for me.

I figured I was texting Bennet, but the message came back:

(317) xxx-xxxx: Who's this?

Me: Riggle

(317) xxx-xxxx: Oh, bennet texted you. Not in class 2gether now though

Me: Sorry

(317) xxx-xxxx: What's the street?

Me: Schort Way.

A little time passed.

(317) xxx-xxxx: Wait why don't you look it up on your own?

Me: Bennet used all my data, and my uncle would kick my ass

(317) xxx-xxxx: Bennet does that.

Whoever it was sent me a picture of a Google map, and Schort Way was at the south side of town.

Brian Allen Carr

I didn't know what time it was, so I got dressed and headed out.

The last time I saw my uncle, he was smoking a Swisher Sweet on the sidewalk, looking up at ragged clouds. "When I was a kid," he said, "your grandpa smoked. A ton. We'd drive around in his station wagon and he'd have beers and cigarettes and we'd listen to Cubs games on the radio, and I was so young that I thought weird things. Like, I sat on the passenger side, and he'd be blowing his smoke out his window, and in my head it was like all that smoke floated up and got caught in the sky. Like it hung there and became the clouds. And I'd watch him smoking. And I'd look at the clouds. And I'd see things in the clouds, you know? The way kids do. Bears and horses and shit. And I'd tell Dad, blow me an elephant. And he'd be like what? And I guess somehow I explained it to him. Because it became our thing. He'd take a big hit off his cigarette," my uncle took a big hit off his cigar and puffed a mess of smoke toward the sky, "and he'd say, here comes a Cubby. Like the mascot. And he'd blow that smoke out his window, and I'd get to looking in the sky for whatever it was he said he blew."

"Ever see it?" I said. "The Cubby?"

"Hell," my uncle said. "People always see what they want to see."

I was walking through Opioid, on my way to Schort Way, when I spotted the Bicycling Confederate standing on a corner with his bike between his legs. I wanted to ask him about Remote again, but something in me just made me see his flag and made me think how bizarre it was that a half-delayed Hoosier would snag such a crummy symbol and devote his life to it.

"Struggler," I hollered at him. "Struggler."

He looked up at me, a sort of spooky blankness in his face, a kind of slack to his mouth, sleep in his eyes. "Who me?"

Now, I don't advocate hitting anyone. I don't. This is mainly because I've been hit before, but it's also because if you hate somebody that much, why would you want them on you?

And I mean, if you beat somebody up they get on you. Their blood and spit. Their skin. Their sweat. We show violence as so dreamy in the movies. Even when people bleed it glistens like sex. Folks will fight a dozen people and never roll an ankle, never sprain a wrist. Go punch a punching bag with no gloves on and see how long you can do it before you start crying.

In *Black Panther* those Wakandan bros swung their fists at everything and everybody. I get T'Challa. Dude's swallowed the Black Panther magic, but what about everyone else? Charge into some terrible fight, then run a mile to fight some other fight? No one ever gets tired, has to shit, needs a drink. The only thing they ever do is crack their necks. That right there, to me, seems to be a flaw. If you need to adjust your spine then you can twist your ankle. It only makes sense. And they're always glistening. Beads of sweat just pouring of them. If you can sweat, you can get thirsty.

I guess I hit the Bicycling Confederate about six times, once I caught up to him. The first two shots landed in his right eye, and then maybe the rest hit his shoulders and the crown of his head and the knuckles of my right hand broke open, and I was bleeding wherever else I stuck him, so I didn't know if had gotten him good, or if I was just bathing him in my own blood, but he dipped out like a kicked puppy, covered his head with his hands and ran off down an alley with his noggin leading the way. I didn't wait long. I pulled the flag from his bike and sailed it like a spear in his direction, jumped on the bicycle and pedaled away.

My dad gave me my first bike. It was one of the best things I could remember about him. He had come home from a route one day and for some reason his semi was parked on the street. At least that's how I remember it. My mom took me out to see him in the front yard, and she was like, "You brought the rig home?"

"Had to," he said. "Got special cargo in the back."

My dad wears navy Dickies in all my memories, and he always has on a plain white T-shirt. He had a few tattoos on his forearms, but I don't remember what they were of. So, in my mind they change all the time. But, in my mind, he always smells like coffee and car trips.

"Special cargo?" my mom said.

"For you and the little man. You my little man, right? Were you good?" I nodded. "Was he good?" he asked my mom, and she held up her hand and waggled it like so-so.

"Gave you the shakes?" my dad asked.

"Shut up," Mom said. It's my best memory of her smile.

He picked me up and held me to him, and threw his arm around my mom, and my mom kissed him and we stumbled over to the back of his rig, and my dad set me down and fished a giant key ring from his pocket. It jangled and clanged. He thumbed through them, found the right key, undid a lock on the roll-up door and told me to close my eyes.

I did.

"And cover them with your hands."

I did.

"And cover his hands with your hands."

My mom did.

I heard the door shimmy its way open, and then my dad said, "You can look now."

My mom took her hands off my hands. I took my hands off my eyes. And when they were open, there was a bike for me sitting lonely in the giant cargo space, and there was a package for my mother, but I don't remember what she got.

I do remember, though, how much our excitement echoed in the empty cargo space whooping and hollering and all, and my dad said, "Don't say I never . . ." He shook his head. "I always forget how that saying goes."

"Gave you a bike," my mom said.

"Yeah," my dad said. "Don't say I never gave you a bike."

And I spent the rest of the afternoon riding up and down the street with my training wheels.

My mom took them off after Dad died. The training wheels. But I don't really remember learning to ride without them. I think one day, I could just do it on my own.

But there I was in Opioid, Indiana, a struggler on a stolen bicycle with the wind in my hair, my hands numb from the cold, snot leaking down my face, the houses whipping by. I rode out to the edge of town, through cornfields dead with winter, along streets glazed with salt and snowmelt. They looked near silver, the roads. Twinkled like sweaty skin. And the air was huge. And above, clouds hung like exhaled smoke. And I tried to find my grandfather's shapes in them.

If the events of it all hadn't been so awkward, I think I would have been having a good time.

Schort Way was a crooked little street with three houses on it. Two seemed straight out of a catalog for suburban dream living, but the third looked like a cavity in a mouth otherwise empty of teeth. The rest of the road was nothing but a stretch of abandonment, a curved thing dotted with broken corn-stalk patches, but I biked up and down it a few times thinking about what to do. There were cars in the driveways of the two nice houses. The other house seemed deserted, and I figured it was the house the waiter was talking about.

The land sloped toward the house. It seemed to heave up like castaway blankets—a janky thing of spent and splintering boards. I got off the bike in the front yard, leaned it to the earth, and the front tire spun the way front tires do, coughing off salt water until it came to a still.

"Hello," I called. As though someone might hear me. I stared up at the windows of the second story. They looked like haunted eyes. Like an old person staring off, trying to remember something. "I'm looking for my uncle," I hollered up again, moving toward the house. And then I wondered what I would even say. If someone came to the door, opened it and was like, "Looking for who? Your junkie uncle? You don't say."

But of course there was no one home. In the yard, there was a FOR SALE BY OWNER sign that looked pretty new. There was also a sign closer to the house that said TRESPASSERS WILL BE SHOT. That sign looked old as hell. Weather broken. Like it had seen a couple dozen winters and summers, and the letters seemed to bleed out at the edges, lose definition and fade off.

I went to the door. I knocked. My knocking seemed to sink away into a vacuum. Nothing stirred. No dogs barked. No footsteps. I knocked again and I watched the windows to see if any of the curtains moved. I knocked again and I decided the house was empty.

I walked around back. The house must have sat on a half-dozen acres. The yard behind it was tree free, and the sun hung bright in the sky. There was a back door and I knocked on it, but I got the same results as in front except this time my shadow was cut crisp against the side of the house, and I flashed Remote against the house. "Schort Way," he said.

"But ain't nobody here."

"Not my problem," he told me, and I put him away.

I looked out toward the sun. At the far edge of the land there was a hedgerow of trees I didn't know the names of. Leafless things on account of winter. The limbs of them clustered together like noise.

I turned back to the house. I put my hand on the doorknob and twisted my wrist. It was unlocked. I leaned into it a bit, and the hinges coughed open, and the door swung into a dark and lonely abode. I stood there in the kitchen and breakfast nook. But there was no table or anything. The countertops were ancient. The linoleum floor seemed gummy. The refrigerator was a shape they don't make anymore. My shadow cut across the room. Up to my waist was across the floor, the rest of me climbed a wall. My head was where my head would be if I was standing with my back to the wall, and I kind of looked my shadow in the eyes. It didn't say anything, and I didn't either.

In the movies death has a terrible smell. Well, in certain kinds of movies. I guess in most movies people just die and the action goes on. But old death, detective-contemplated death, where, like, seasoned investigators cover their faces with a rag and new recruits puke at the crime scene—in those movies death is stinky. But I guess, owing to it being winter, my uncle didn't stink. I found him in the living room. The second room I entered. The sun from the kitchen hung in shafts and dust danced in the otherwise stillness of the light, and it was like these odd corridors, and my uncle was sitting in a beam of it, his dead-opened eyes twinkling, his teeth shining in his frozen-opened mouth.

There is nothing more still than dead people. I knew that from finding my mom. They seem so far away when you touch them. Like all the life they once had has retreated down to live in the marrow of their bones, but you can still feel the energy of it down there burning. Like a hot coal sunk down in mounds of ash the morning after a campfire. And the surface of them feels bizarre, because it's not warm like it should be, not soft like it should be. The only thing like it is taxidermied deer. The kind that hunters hang the heads of on walls.

My uncle's pants were frozen with piss, the wood floor around him too.

I kneeled to him and touched his chest. His clothes seemed miles above his lifelessness.

I'd heard of cats dying with meows in their throats. Like you'd go to pick up a dead cat, and the jostling of its dead body would purge one final, bungled meow that slips from their mouths clumsily. And I pressed on my uncle's chest, I guess, and a sort of "humph" purged from him, but I smelled his frozen breath.

All of a sudden, the reality of it came shocking through the room. The whole place seemed to gag. Like the universe was puking. And I stood up and bounced back from my uncle, the dust rushing in the light now because of my disturbing it.

"Fucking A," I told myself. I put my hands on my face. I thought and thought.

The biggest difference between Opioid, Indiana, and South Texas was timing. Well, and weather. Well, and the language and the color of the people. But there were tons of similarities. People were just people, you know. They came and went, they had children they loved. Yards they mowed. Things they hated. They ate food. They listened to music. I know these are trivial things, except they really aren't. They hung US flags from their houses on Memorial Day. They went to church on Easter. Again, I know, but I don't know.

Opioid, Indiana, had happened. It had risen and gleamed but then it had fallen. You could tell it by the sag in the houses, the grit on the street signs. You could tell it by the slack faces on the dawdling junkies. You could tell it in the gray of the days. South Texas, on the other hand, was popping off. All the homes seemed to be fresh out of candy wrappers. All the streets seemed to sit new on the earth. The mall was clean. The bathrooms in houses weren't drippy.

Opioid, Indiana, had a yesterday feel. South Texas seemed primed for tomorrow.

I don't know how long my uncle had been dead, but he was longer dead than my mom had been when I found her. I thought that thought and wondered, who my age has done that before? Measured the death of one dead relative against another by the way they felt when you found them.

I was happy, though, that my uncle wasn't the first dead person I'd found. And then I thought: *Totally healthy thought to think. You won't have to work this out in therapy ever.*

My phone vibrated and I checked my texts.

(317) xxx-xxxx: Find that place?

Me: I'll tell you when you tell me who you are.

(317) xxx-xxxx: Bennet my struggler.

Me: Then tell me whose phone.

(317) xxx-xxxx: She made me promise.

Me: Then I got secrets too.

I held my phone and dropped on a knee next to my uncle, and I looked at my uncle, and then I looked at my phone. I was trying to decide what I should do.

I had options.

1. I could call the cops. This seemed like a not great idea for a few reasons.
   a. I had never called the cops before, and I wasn't sure if on cell phones you just dialed 911 or what.
   b. I didn't know if I was allowed to be out and about when suspended.
   c. What would I even tell them? That I'd found my days-old dead uncle who'd been missing for a stretch of time but who we hadn't yet called the cops over?
2. I could call Peggy, but what would I say to her? My gawd. It might be harder to talk to her about it than it would be to call the cops.
3. I could text Peggy. But what would I text?
   a. "Found Uncle"
   b. "Uncle dead"
   c. A picture of his dead ass?
4. I could leave. I could pretend I didn't see anything. I could go home and just act like nothing had happened. Like I'd never seen a thing.

I decided on option four. I think it was because it was the least work and because it meant I didn't have to blame myself for whatever happened. I mean, everything up to that point had nothing to do with me. I hadn't made any decisions. I hadn't done anything. So, I decided that what I'd seen, I hadn't seen. That it wasn't real at all. That I would continue on like normal, and I headed for the door, but my phone jiggled in my pocket.

I checked it.

(317) xxx-xxxx: Can you pay me back for Black Panther. I'm broke. Moms is being stingy this month.
Me: Shit, I'm broker.

And I was. I had gotten paid from the gig at Broth, but now what the hell would Peggy and I even do. If there was a Peggy and I. Like, if my uncle was dead, I'd probably just get shipped off again. I looked back at my uncle crumpled against the wall.

"Don't fuck up, huh?"

I don't know, I got angry, and I walked back toward him, and I think I was about to put a shoe to his face, but then something dawned on me: I should check his pockets. It's what they always did in movies. Someone dies, you check to see what they got.

So, I dropped down to my uncle and started putting my hands in his clothes.

Nothing feels more bizarre than the pants pockets of a dead man. It's a weird, unfortunate space. I went in and out of everything until I came to his wallet. It was fat with cash. There were some pills in his other pockets, but I didn't want any part of that. And his phone lay beside him deader than him.

I counted the bills. It was about $1,300. Enough for rent and some more. It felt weird, the money. Like old leaves. Like the skin of something mounted.

The rest of the afternoon, I rode around on the streets through the cornfields. I didn't know where to go. I just pedaled until the cold didn't bother me anymore, until I couldn't feel a thing.

Now, here's a thing I guess I didn't think through. The Bicycling Confederate really loved his bicycle, and when you get your bicycle stolen, you go looking for it. Also, the dude had family. I figured he had sprung from earth. Like he rose up one year from a cornfield fully formed and emerged from the crops just before the combines swept across the lands, with his bicycle in tow and his flag already flying.

I was out at the edge of Opioid, cruising, watching the sun crawl across the sky, breathing in the fresh farm air and letting my time pass. I'm not great at describing cold. It's a newer sensation to me. I know heat like I know my skin. It holds you as if in manipulated time. A time that is slowed. A time that you meld with. You hover in it. Your molecules seem to stretch into a summer day, into a 100-degree scenario. Your water, the thing you are the most, abandons you to join the manipulated time. Your insides bubble to the top of you, purge and steam away against gravity. You pass through the shirt you're wearing. You evaporate into the atmosphere.

But cold? What does it really do? It clenches you. Your skin tightens away from low temperatures. You shrink and pucker. You dry up to ash. It's supposed to be that the molecules stand still. But that's not how it feels. Your hands race with ache. Your fingers tingle.

Fingers never tingle in the heat.

It's a collapsing, the cold.

If your body was a city in the cold, the buildings would implode.

If your body was a city in the heat, the buildings would launch like rocket ships and streak out across the sky.

All of this was spinning through my mind when an old F-250 pulled up and a shotgun was pointed at my head.

"Get the fuck off that bicycle," someone said, and I hit the brakes.

Now, no one will teach you this, but if someone points a gun at your head, you have to pretend like it's no big deal.

The best rapper from Texas, which makes him one

of the best rappers in the world, is Scarface. I knew how to handle the situation because of him. In "I'm Dead" on *Mr. Scarface Is Back* he tells a story about a crazy guy who stabbed someone with a knife just because their eyes showed fear.

So, inside I was shitting my pants, which is a weird sensation when you're on a bicycle, but outwardly I just kind of looked over at the guy who was holding the gun at my head and said, "Who me?"

"You see another motherfucker on a bicycle?"

I looked around. "Nah?"

"Willy, get out the truck and get your shit."

The guy in the back seat of the driver's side was the one talking at me, pointing the gun at me. The windows of the truck were deeply tinted, and I couldn't see who was driving.

"In the old days they hanged horse thieves," the guy told me.

"This ain't a horse," I told him.

He chambered a round, which meant two things:

1. Up until then I was relatively safe.
2. After that, I was a finger waggle away from being a headless struggler.

"Ain't much different though," he said.

The Bicycling Confederate had gotten down off the truck and he'd come around to get his bike back.

"Hey, Willy," I said to him. I got off his bike and he took it away.

"I think we should hang him," said Willy. "Like in the old days," he said.

"Well, in the old days they woulda shot you for your Confederate flag for sure. If we're, like, gonna be all old days about it."

"Fuck off, faggot," the gun holder said. "Bet you voted Hillary."

"I'm seventeen."

Willy, he looked different when he wasn't on his bicycle with his flag flapping. I kind of felt sorry for him. But then he screamed, "Shoot him!"

"Calm down, Willy," said the gun holder. "You got your bike."

"He hit me though."

The gun holder shrugged. "Put your bike in the bed," he told Willy, and Willy did.

The street was still. I was quiet. The F-250 idled chuggingly. The exhaust of it pumping away into the frozen air, floating out toward the winterized cornfields.

Once Willy was back in the truck, they drove away.

———

Walking after you get off a bicycle seems slow as fuck. The streets that would have streaked by earlier just tumbled beneath my feet, and the slow progress of it all got me thinking about my uncle. And my mother. And father. And me.

Was it me?

Did I make them all die?

Listen, I'm not a good student but I know about causality, and I've read plenty of books. I've watched plenty of smart YouTube videos. Sometimes when I should've been doing homework. I understand relativity. I understand that time is a concept we've both invented and that exists. That it changes depending on where you are. That the present is not as simple as you'd think. That memories aren't trustworthy.

People around me die.

They die for different reasons, but the outcome is the same.

My dad died from working an unsafe job. My mom died from pain. My uncle died from trying not to feel pain.

And maybe all of those are the same sort of thing.

Like, there's no way my father wanted to be a truck driver. There's no way my mom wanted to be a widow raising a child alone. There's no way my uncle wanted to be what he was.

Was I the cause, somehow, for the deaths of everyone around me?

My dad probably just drove trucks so he could do things like buy me bicycles. My mom probably felt overwhelmed by life, because she would have to raise me on her own. My uncle only had the money to OD because he got my checks.

And it was a painfully cold walk, because the outside matched my insides. All gray and frozen. All despair and salted surfaces.

Peggy spoke the moment I opened the apartment door.

"Anything?" she asked.

My cheeks felt like oysters and they stung when I got into the heated room. My hands burned in the warmth. "Nah," I told her. "I'm tired."

"Wait," she said, "I've been thinking . . ."

But I brushed past her and went to my room. I got in bed. I wanted to sleep it all away.

Then a knock came at the window. I went to open it. I knew it was Bennet.

"You got that money?"

"Yeah, hang on," I told him.

"Man, you look sad or something."

"Rough day." I went for my pants to get him his cash.

"What you need is some curly carrot leaf?" He looked at me with his bald head.

"Nah, I'm good."

"Know what, man, fuck it. I don't need the money. Keep it."

"It's cool. Let me get it."

"Nah, nah." He touched his head. "I can't wait till this shit grows back."

"Yeah," I told him. "You look better with hair."

"Wanna know something?" he told me.

"What?"

"You're my best friend," he said.

I sort of looked at him. He was crouched there at the window. "What's that about?"

"I don't know. Just thought about it. See ya," he said. And then he was gone.

"You too," I said to the spot where he used to be.

Friday

H̲ere's how Remote says Friday got its name:

When the rain of Thirstday finally stopped, the world had gone mud messy, and Remote couldn't do anything without getting dirty.

"*This is the worst,*" *Remote said. I picked up my foot and looked at the clumps that clung to it.* "*It's almost as bad as being thirsty.*"

Current problems are always worse than the problems you've solved. Remote sat in the muck and stared off at the puddles and grime. Remote couldn't get motivated. Remote's life seemed like a disaster.

But just then, a woman I had never met waltzed into my village. She had a unibrow, and she was dressed in vivid colors, and she had an angry posture, and her hands were artist's hands. "*Is it true,*" *the woman said,* "*that you have the power to name days?*"

Remote thought. Was it a power I had? Was it anything?

"*Maybe,*" *said I.* "*Depends who's asking.*"

The woman raised her chin. "*I am Frida,*" *she said,* "*and I can fix your troubles.*"

"*How?*" *Remote asked. I grabbed a fistful of mud, and squeezed it so that it dripped through my fingers.* "*This stuff is everywhere.*"

"*Correct,*" *said Frida,* "*but you can solve sadness with work.*"

"*Sadness?*" *said Remote, holding open my dirty palm.* "*That's what you'd call this?*"

"*That I'd call mud,*" *said Frida.* "*But the way*

it makes you feel. How you're staring off at nothing and feeling sorry for yourself. That I'd call sadness. But all you have to do with sadness is remember that everything passes. To know that all things can yield other things." Frida waved her hand over the earth, and a hibiscus sprang from the spot she had gestured to, and great hibiscus flowers as wide as dinner plates bloomed. They were the most brilliant pink imaginable.

"No mud," said Frida. "No flowers. You have to focus on how the pain of now can lead to the joy of tomorrow."

"So you'll turn all this mud into flowers?"

"Of course not," said Frida.

Remote became sadder.

"We'll turn the mud into flowers together." Frida stroked her unibrow. "I have seeds for us all."

Frida passed out pouches to Remote and the Earthlings and we waddled through the mud scattering seeds.

In time, flowers grew. Once the flowers came, the earth was dry again. To commemorate our hero, we named the day Friday.

And Friday became the day to celebrate the end of the sadness. To listen to music. To go out. To enjoy the evening.

———

I lay in bed looking at the scabs on my knuckles and every now and then I counted the money I'd found in my uncle's wallet. Money is so weird. In jail, people hide it up their asses. They call that a prison wallet. If a kid loses a tooth, you put a bill beneath their pillow. That bill could've been up someone's butt a week before, could've passed through the hands of meth dealers who'd murdered people. And then that kid takes it to buy candy.

I don't know.

I was going to be washing dishes that night at Broth, and I didn't want to do much. I wanted all my energy to be saved. I knew once I got out of bed, I'd pace around. My nerves would start to work. I'd burn myself out from the inside.

What would I tell Peggy? What would she do after she knew? What would they do to me? Where would I go then?

I tried to sleep the day away, but I just lay there looking at the texture of the ceiling. I texted Erika that I missed her, but she didn't text back. I texted the unknown number that Bennet had texted from, but it didn't text back. It's weird waiting for that kind of communication. Because you don't know what's been seen and ignored, and you don't know what hasn't been seen yet.

You start to make things up. You start to imagine the worst. Maybe Erika didn't miss me back. Maybe the person who had the unknown phone was just laughing at me.

I picked up my philosophy book and read about another philosopher. I read about Epicurus. He was a hedonist. He wanted to know why people were happy or unhappy. Everyone thought that he was kind of a wild dude. That he banged virgins and drank all day. Ate whatever. Did nothing but dance. But that's not the way he was. He studied happiness, but he was real chill about it. He ate almost nothing. Just enough to keep himself alive. He only owned a few pairs of clothes. He said people make three big mistakes when they think of happiness. He said people think happiness is this:

1. Sex
2. Money
3. Luxury

Which is kind of like that song of Drake's called "Successful." He wants money, cars, clothes and hoes. Epicurus said, though, that those things don't mean shit. Epicurus would've looked at Drake and called him a miserable motherfucker. And if you think about it, maybe it's true. Go watch Drake giving Rihanna the Vanguard Award. It might be the saddest shit on the internet.

Instead, Epicurus said that what you really want is:

1. Friends
2. A job you enjoy
3. Time to think

Can you imagine if Drake sang:

I want some people
People who I like
A job that's alright
And time
To unwind
I just wanna be successful

Dude wouldn't sell shit. He'd be back in the Six, and maybe he'd be the happiest motherfucker alive.

When I got up to shower, Peggy was gone. I knew rent was due, so I put the eight hundred dollars on the kitchen table, texted her that I'd left money, and then headed to work.

On the way, I saw Autistic Ross, and I went up to him to see if he had any answers.

"You boy," he said to me. "We talked afore. The other day. About right here." He looked around on his little spot. He had on a pink Polo shirt and he was wearing navy slacks. He pulled his elbows up at his sides and he smiled big and squirreled around some. "Talked Alaska," he told me. "Talked the dadgum weather," he said. His top teeth dangled out of his grin.

"That's right," I told him. His joy was infectious. His words seemed to cleanse me. "I had a question for you?"

"For me? You gonna ask if I'm cold? I'm about to go get my jacket on," he said. "Beyond that I am generally lacking when it comes to the answers department. Momma use to say I'd forget my name if it was any longer than Ross. But I like Ross better than any other name anyhow, but I couldn't tell you why. Ain't that funny how you never really know why you like what you like. Like I like creamy peanut butter better than crunchy peanut butter, but if you chew on crunchy peanut butter a bit, it gets real creamy in your mouth. Maybe I just don't like all that dadgum work."

Everything he said made sense, but I swear you got stupider just following his lines of thought. "When I came by the other day you showed me something?"

"I showed you where the body's buried?" He had a shocked look on his face.

"What?" I said.

He cackled. "That's my little joke. I tell it different

ways. Sometimes people say, 'Wanna know a secret?' and I say, 'I know where the body's buried.'" His eyes watered. "The way I just told it to you. I ain't never told it quite that way before. Maybe you can teach an old dog new tricks."

"Maybe," I told him. I could feel my brain shrinking. I held up Remote.

"I know that fella." He held up his hand like mine.

"Yeah," I told him. "Where'd you learn that."

"Promised not to tell," he said. "And Ross don't break no promises. I break wind sometimes though." He kinda leaned to one side and clenched his face. "It was a quiet one," he said. "Oh, boy, it's smelly though."

"What the fuck?" The stench was insane. "What do you eat?"

"Sausage," he told me. "Peanut butter. Raisins."

"Fucking rank," I said and I started to walk off.

"Come again," he told me, and I swear the smell followed me a half a mile.

At Broth, the banging around had started, and I jumped into my apron and filled up my sinks. There wasn't much to wash, but there was a lot of stuff to run back. There were stacks of plates, pans to shelve. There were forks and spoons and knives to wipe clean. They had to be spotless.

Chef showed me a spoon and was like, "Would you put that in your mouth?'

I looked at it. "Sure."

She held it closer to me. There were spots on it, I guess. "Sure, Chef. But that's old dishwater," she said. "That's about as bad as dried sweat. Would you lick my armpits?"

"Are they shaved?"

Chef laughed. "You're a fucking gem," she said. "Spotless spoons," she told me. "Spotless forks. Spotless knives. Spotless everything."

"Spotless armpits," I told her.

"Spotless armpits, Chef."

It's weird when you look at a tub of forks and realize that every single one of those is going to go into a different person's mouth. At home, those forks and spoons you have go into five people in an average cycle. The forks and spoons at a restaurant go into dozens of people in a night.

I thought about that as I was getting rid of all the spots. That everything I was cleaning was going to be inside somebody soon.

The waiter who had given me the ride came up as I was polishing the silverware. "Moving spots?" he said.

"Huh?"

"Matter can't be created or destroyed."

"Okay."

"You think you're getting rid of the spots, but you aren't. You're moving them." He pointed to the silverware. "From there," he pointed to the towel I was holding, "to there."

"Chef," I hollered. "Washing dishes blows my mind."

"Oh, it blows," she called back.

That afternoon, a storm came through and we caught four inches of accumulation, and we only had three tables all night. Almost everything I had thought before was a lie. My silverware barely went into anybody.

"Can't trust this Indiana weather," Chef said.

She saw my knuckle. The warm water from the sinks had made it open back up. "What happened?"

"I caught it on something."

"Health inspector sees that and we'd get cited for sure. Let's wrap it up."

She took me into the office and pulled a first aid kit down from a bookshelf full of cookbooks. "You read at all?" she asked, I guess having seen me eye the shelves.

"Yeah," I told her. "I'm reading about Epicurus."

"The food site?"

"Nah, the philosopher."

"This is gonna sting." She had an alcohol pad that she rubbed over my wound, and it felt hot and cold at the same time and my eyes clenched. "Would you read a food book if I gave it to you?"

"Sure," I said. I gritted my teeth. "Eventually."

"This lady's my hero." She reached up and grabbed a book called *Blood, Bones & Butter*. I took it in my good hand, and Chef took back my right hand and put a butterfly bandage over the split knuckle and smoothed it over. My mom was the last person who'd held my hand. I'd hooked up with some girls, but I hadn't held hands with anyone, and definitely not like this. Chef held my hand like she felt sorry for it. Like it meant something to her to help me, and it occurred to me that I was going to read the book she gave me and that the woman who wrote it would be one of my heroes too. Then Chef handed me a latex glove. "Hand condom," she told me. "No knuckle AIDS for you."

I put it on. "Thanks, Chef," I told her.

"De nada," she said. "Now get to fucking work."

A slow shift in a restaurant and a busy shift in a restaurant might as well be two different jobs. I had hoped my night at Broth would take away my time to think, would fold me into its insanity and the hours would go streaking by. Instead, we all waited tensely in the kitchen for customers who never came. Listening to the energy of the kitchen purr.

"Fucking lame," hollered Chef.

She started cutting the servers. She had the cooks kick me all the dishes they didn't need. The kitchen was dismantled into a skeleton configuration. The chattering of it sounded like machinery. All the hotel pans consolidated, all the elements of the line shifted down to one station. Chef had me take everything out of the walk-in cooler. She had me wipe down the surfaces. She had me put everything back.

"Imma spell a word," Chef told me, "and you tell me what it spells."

"Okay."

"*C-H-E-V-R-E.*"

I thought a second. "Cheaver," I said.

Chef smiled. "Shev-ra," she told me. "It's a cheese. Ever had it?"

"Nah."

She opened a container, took a plastic spoon from her pocket and spooned me a taste.

"You always have spoons in your pocket, Chef?"

"Always. I need to get away from plastic though. I need to find some wood ones or something. They're great for tasting, but they say by 2050 there'll be more trash in the ocean than fish. By weight," she said. "But try it."

"It looks like cream cheese," I told her.

"It's goat though."

"It's goat?"

"Well, goat's milk cheese. So it doesn't taste like cream cheese. And cream cheese isn't really cheese anyhow. And we wouldn't use it in my kitchen. Neufchâtel maybe."

"Noof-sha-what?"

"We'll get to it. Try the chèvre."

I did. The little bite of it took over my mouth. The wallop of it was astounding. It was hideously creamy. It was disgustingly delicious. "It tastes like how river water smells."

"Like it?"

I swallowed. "Afterwards tastes like change," I told her.

"Change?"

"Money," I said.

"Metallic," she said. "It's local. See? You learned something."

I threw away my spoon.

When I was done cleaning the walk-in, I started scrubbing away at what all the cooks brought me.

My glove kept filling up with water, and it kept

breaking, and after I'd changed it a few times, I decided it was a waste.

Eventually, my Band-Aid got lost in the dishwater, and if I bled on anything, I just sprayed the blood away.

There was one table left late in the evening, and the conspiracy-theory waiter kept coming in and rolling his eyes. "If they tip well," he said, "I don't mind. But I hate working this late for one table."

"They're drinking though, right?" said Chef.

"Like fish, Chef."

"Then let 'em stay."

The waiter went back out to the dining room and came back a bit later with a dessert order. "And," he said handing the order to Chef, "they want to know if they can see the kitchen."

I'd never even heard of that, but apparently it's a thing. Especially in nicer restaurants. People want to get pictures of themselves with cooks, they want to see where their food came from.

"We're pretty broken down," said Chef. "But as long as you tell them, I don't mind."

I had filled a mop bucket the way I'd been shown on my first shift, and I was about to go over the kitchen floor. Normally, we would've scrubbed the floors with a long-handled brush first, but the night was so slow Chef said we didn't need to.

"Hang back on mopping a bit," she told me. She went into her office and grabbed a fresh jacket, took off her hat and messed her hair a bit. "I look okay?" she asked.

She did.

It occurred to me then, I liked women. I didn't like girls. I liked Peggy and I liked Chef. I liked them physically, but there was something more than that. They had power over me, they had control. Peggy could have kicked me out onto the street and Chef could have fired me, and something about that was interesting. They could also teach me. They knew things I didn't know. And I'm not sure that's what men are supposed to like, but you can't help what you're into.

I mean, I knew plenty of girls who dated older boys. Hell, they almost all did. Part of that was because the older boys had cars, but maybe there was something else to it.

It used to be more common for men to date women a lot younger. I think these days it's more frowned on. But maybe the men like younger women for the same reason I liked Chef. Just because. They liked girls who needed their money. They liked girls who they were smarter than. Who they had power over, and maybe those women liked that the men had power. Liked they had money. Liked they had knowledge.

It's weird how society makes decisions for us. How

society tells us how to feel about what we like—about what we're like.

If I told my friends that I was into Chef, they would tease me. If I told my friends that I had a girlfriend two years younger than me, they'd think it was cool. But where do all the lines start and stop, and why do we have to carry the opinion of the world on our eyes like lenses?

I suppose you have to have some boundaries. You have to tell men they can't fall in love with seven-year-olds. You have to tell women high school teachers they can't sleep with their students. You have to tell bosses they can't fire employees for refusing them blow jobs. I don't know. It's confusing. All of it.

I barely recognized her when she came to the back because her mouth was blue from drinking wine and her eyes looked wonky, but she recognized me right away.

"I know you," the kitchen visitor told me, wagging her finger. She was wearing heels and she kinda stumbled a bit, but the conspiracy-theory waiter steadied her, and then she reached down and took off a heel. It was my counselor. The one who had pinned the vape on me.

"It's not the safest place to go barefoot," Chef told her.

"Where's the chef?" my counselor said.

You could feel a kind of temperature change, and Chef said, "Gone for the evening."

And the counselor looked at the waiter and said, "But you said . . ."

"Just stepped out," I said. "Just like right now." I pointed to the back door. "Had to go see . . ."

"A man about a man thing," said Chef. "Y'know," she said. "Men."

My counselor nodded heavily. "You can't count on 'em," she said. She pointed at me. "This one's kinda trouble."

"I hope so," said Chef. "This is a kitchen. We only hire trouble."

"Weed smoker," said my counselor. "Vape pen."

"Vaping's not smoking," Chef said.

"True," said the counselor. "He had a funny word for it. What was that funny word?"

"Candy fog."

"Sounds like a stripper," Chef said.

"His mom didn't think it was funny," my counselor said. "I told her what you wanna be when you grow up."

"You mean my aunt?" I asked the counselor.

"Some woman," she said. "She said you'd be lucky to be that bicycle guy. That you'd be lucky to be homeless. She didn't think you'd live long enough. I figured she was gonna kill you."

"I'm still here," I said.

My counselor looked around a bit. "Well I've seen it," she said to the waiter. "Food was AH-MAZING."

"Thanks," said Chef.

Then the waiter helped her back to the dining room.

"No wonder kids shoot up schools," Chef said once the counselor was gone.

At a certain point it gets so cold you can't even tell you're alive anymore. That night was like that—standing outside made you feel like you'd crumble to dust and drift off with the snow—but I didn't want to ride with the conspiracy-theory waiter. My pants were wet, and my shirt was soaked, but I bundled into my jacket and threw up my hood, and I waded through the snowbanks wondering why people liked winter. And some people did. I knew that some folks watched the weather for blizzards and kind of had blizzard parties the way we'd have hurricane parties back on the Texas coast.

In 2015 my last guardian bought extra beer for Hurricane Bill and I was only fifteen but he let me drink with him. We didn't get much more than rain. Too far south. But we sat on the back porch under the easement in candlelight slurping Lone Stars, and he told some ghost stories, but none of them stuck with me. It's weird how some things you remember and some things you forget. And it's weird how you don't get to decide. You can't trim away things from your brain that you wish weren't there, and you can't dig out the memories that seem lost forever. Your brain shows you what it wants you to see. Your mind is totally at its mercy.

The snow was stacked like white scabs and the streetlights hummed yellow in the hiss of new snow falling. Flakes the size of my thumbnail. They drifted down, and their silence seemed to slow the whole world.

I felt cold enough to die but I knew I wouldn't. We'd read a story earlier that year in English about a man up in Alaska, I think. He had a dog, and he needed to start a fire but couldn't. And he kept worrying that it was 50 degrees below. At a point, to keep his hands warm, he thought of slicing open the dog, of burying his hands in dog guts the way Han Solo kept Luke Skywalker warm inside a tauntaun on Hoth. But it wasn't 50 degrees below, so dogs were safe near me and my hands.

Peggy had known about my being suspended. She knew about the Bicycling Confederate and Autistic Ross too and how I said I wanted to be like them. She knew about the vape pen. She knew about Remote.

But she said she didn't.

And I guess in my shock of all that, and in the pain from my uncle, my mind started going funny places. I could see, somehow, in my mind a vast puzzle being pieced together. A weird conspiracy against me. My aunt somehow planning all these things. My uncle's death. My seeing Remote on other people's hands. And I didn't know why, but I just knew she was deceiving me.

The apartment lights were on when I finally got home, and Peggy sat cross-legged on the sofa. She wasn't doing anything. You could tell she was waiting for me, but she didn't know what I knew, and because of that I had power over her, and she didn't seem nearly as sexy as she sat in the warm light.

When I went inside, she shot up to her feet. "You leave that money on the table?" she asked.

"I did."

"Where'd you get it?"

"Like you don't know?"

"You think I'd ask if I did?"

I went to the refrigerator and opened it up. There were some beers that my uncle kept around, but he never would let me drink in the apartment. He didn't want me to become like him. I grabbed a bottle and twisted off the cap.

"You know what your uncle thinks of that," Peggy said, and she made to come and take the beer from me.

But I said, "I know what he *thought* about it."

Peggy and I locked eyes.

"What do you mean?"

I took a swig of beer. The bottle kind of hooted when I pulled it from my mouth, and I wiped my lips with my busted knuckle, my tongue numbing in the alcohol wash. "It's called past tense."

"I know what it is. Where's your uncle?"

"Why are you lying?" I asked. "How do you know about Remote?"

Her face clenched. "About what?"

I held my hand up and made Remote. I spoke, and as I did, I had Remote's mouth move with mine. "You knew I was suspended." I widened my eyes. "You knew about the bicyclist and Ross. I saw my counselor tonight, so there's no use in lying. You somehow knew about Remote and you somehow got Ross and the Confederate to play along in your game. I'm not sure why you'd do that, but there can only be a few reasons."

"What the fuck are you even saying?"

"Either you killed him and wanted to pin it on me, or you killed him and wanted me to find him so I'd run away."

"I am literally under the impression that you've lost

your mind or are on acid." She looked at Remote. "What the fuck are you doing with your hand?"

"You're a murderer," Remote and I told her. "You're a killer and you've been lying this whole time." Remote was up near her face, so close she would smell his breath if he had any. "You're twisted and evil, and you've been playing me this whole time."

"What?"

"You talked to her on the phone."

"Who?"

"My counselor."

"When?"

"On Friday."

"I was drunk as fuck on Friday."

"Yeah, had to steady your nerves?" Remote and I said. "Couldn't get over what you'd done? Killer. Murderer."

Peggy slapped Remote and my hand went open. "Killer? Murderer? Are you crazy? Where'd you find the money? Think about it. Where?"

I didn't have to think. "In Uncle Joe's wallet."

"In his fucking wallet," she said. "You think I'd kill someone and not take their money?" She put her face near my face.

"Whatever," I said, and I finished my beer in a few giant pulls. When it was empty, I set the bottle on the counter. "I don't need to talk about it." And I went to my room.

Saturday

Bennet woke me up the next day by tapping at my window. "I got the curly carrot leaf," he said.

"What?"

"C'mon."

I got dressed and climbed out the window. I smelled like dirty dishwater, but I didn't much care. I zipped up my coat and couldn't smell myself as bad. The sun was out, and the fallen snow had a way of making the day warmer. Everything glowed and Opioid, Indiana, seemed like an entirely different place with the weekend crowd roaming around.

I hadn't gone to school in a week, but still Saturday had a vibe. It felt like an unusual and beautiful thing. All the freedom in the roads. All the happy people on their days off drifting about. Kids rolling snowmen. Men shoveling sidewalks. The slick sound of the cars on the streets, turning over snow that coughed and crumbled.

"You alright?" Bennet said.

I guess I was in a daze and I guess he'd been trying to talk to me, but we were just walking to a place to smoke and I had gotten lost in thought.

"Yeah. Yeah."

"Well?"

"Well what?"

"Well where you wanna go smoke this?"

I looked around. "We're tight, right?"

"Yeah. The tightest."

"Like if I asked you to do something but couldn't tell you all about it, you'd come, right?"

"Depends. I mean, what you asking exactly?"

"Will you come with me to see something? And we can smoke there."

"See what?"

"That's what I can't tell you until we get there, but just come."

"How far is it?"

"It's a walk but it's worth it to me."

Bennet was wearing a heavy jacket, and he pulled his hood over his head. "Alright then."

———

I don't know exactly how long it took us to get to Schort Way, but when we got there, Bennet went stiff. "Looks like a fucking trap house."

I looked it over. "I guess it is."

We went around back and Bennet paused harder when we got to the door. "Is it safe?"

"Maybe? I mean, I think. I'm not taking you here because I don't think it's safe. I'm just taking you here because . . . I don't even know why exactly. There's something in there that I've seen, and I'm not sure anyone else has seen it, and I just kind of need you to see it, so someone else has."

"Okay. What is it?"

"I'll show you."

Bennet paused again. "Is there something we gotta do in there?"

"Well, we're gonna smoke, and then we'll talk about it."

"I don't know if I make the best decisions after I've smoked," Bennet said.

"Oh, I make terrible decisions when I'm high. But it doesn't really matter. Whatever we decide will be a bad decision."

"So why we even going in?"

"Because we have to."

We moved through the kitchen and into the living room, and the sun came through the front windows of the house, so you could see the shape of my uncle leaned against the wall, but he rested in shadow, and you couldn't tell he was dead.

"Who's that?" said Bennet. There was caution in his tone.

"My dead uncle," I told him.

"The fuck?" said Bennet, kind of dancing back. "There's a dead motherfucker in here?"

"No," I said, "there's a dead uncle in here. My dead uncle. Light the joint."

"I don't know, man."

"Light the joint."

Bennet rubbed his head and his hair was kind of growing back so you could hear a noise like static. "This is fucked up." He sort of gabbled nothing, and his eyes flickered back and forth.

He lipped the joint, lit it up, puffed some. He took two hits and passed. He was holding in smoke but said, "Super fucked-up," when he passed it to me, his voice strained and throaty.

"I agree." I took my puffs and blew smoke toward my uncle, and I squatted like a baseball catcher so my smoke blew across his lifeless face.

I looked back at Bennet as he blew smoke toward the ceiling. He stood quietly watching it dissipate. He passed back, and we were like that a while. The joint going back and forth between us. The air getting dank and spicy.

After a few turns he went to hand it back to me but I said, "I'm good for now."

"Me too," said Bennet. He half spit into his fingers and clamped his spitty grip down onto the cherry of the thing, and it went out with a mild hiss, and he pocketed what was left. "We'll save it for later," he said. "How long's he been here?"

"I dunno really."

"How'd you find him?"

"I don't really know. How high are you?" I asked.

He looked around the room. "Uh, pretty high, I guess."

I reached my hand up in front of the window where light was shining through, and I made Remote, and Remote flashed in shadow form against the opposite wall. "Ever seen that?"

"What is it?"

"Remote," I said.

"Remote?"

I nodded. "My mom used to show him to me. He was like our thing. A bedtime thing. He'd tell me all kinds of stories."

"Stories?"

"Yeah, like why winter's cold. How the days got their names."

There was no furniture in the room, so Bennet sat on the floor Indian style. "Tell me a story, Remote?" he said at the shadow.

"Ah, man, I don't know about all that."

"C'mon. We just got high with your dead uncle. I don't see any reason why there should be any secrets between us."

I thought a second. "I have to make a voice," I said.

Bennet looked at me. "Huh?"

"He has a kind of voice. Like an accent," I said, nodding toward Remote.

"Well, I should hope so," said Bennet.

"Okay," I said. "Here's how Saturday got its name. But I'm gonna change it a bit, so it makes more sense for you."

Long ago, before time and shadows, Remote began to name the days. He started with Monday. He had named up until Friday. Each day had a specific purpose. Each day had a story that meant something. Monday

was about a killer and his adoptive father. Tuesday was about a great warrior who blew smoke. Wednesday was about a crazy man who caught the sun with an arrow. Thursday was about the disease of thirst. Friday was about working away pain.

But there was a half human named Satur who had no purpose. Think of a thing and he sucked at it. He couldn't dance and he couldn't wage war and he couldn't catch anything and he couldn't keep a job. Still, he wanted a day named after himself. He wanted to be remembered.

Satur came to Remote on the day after Friday, and Remote had been out partying late the night before, and Remote felt like death.

"I want a day named after me," Satur told me. "I like the idea of it. I heard that's what you guys do. How can we make that happen?"

Remote was puking. He could barely think. "What do you do?" Remote asked, and puked in a bush. "What are your gifts?"

"I don't do anything," Satur said proudly. "I just kind of hang around."

Remote considered this. Remote's face was green with nausea. "You couldn't have come at a more perfect time," Remote said. "Today is for just nothing. Nothing at all."

*Satur beamed. He and Remote loafed around
all day.*

*And Saturday became the day for recovery, the
day for waking up late and lounging around and
puking in bushes.*

"That's some crazy shit."

"Yeah, well my dead mom told me that story, so,
y'know . . ."

"I meant that in a good way though."

"Sure."

"I'm serious." Bennet looked at the wall. He looked
back at me. He looked back at the wall. "And who is he
again?"

"Remote."

"What the fuck is that again?"

"It's just a name, I guess."

The walk home was a bizarre mishmash of feels and
weirds. The glint of the sun was beautiful, but my
insides were dead-uncle stained. My brain was a loopy
thing of thoughts. When you're high, you understand
things in a way that makes no sense when you're sober.
You do maths of emotions. You solve puzzles that have
no true pieces.

I was finding answers to questions my mind couldn't give shape to. I was tying together invisible threads too slippery to hold with mental fingers.

Bennet and I had a snowball fight. Bennet and I ran and slid on the road surface. Bennet and I found shapes in the clouds.

"I'll see you later," I said, when we got back to the complex. "Don't tell anyone."

"Tell anyone what?"

Peggy wasn't home, so I sat on the sofa, just waiting. I had to see where her mind was at. I had to see what she thought we should do. I texted her.

Me: We should talk
Peggy: On my way home now

I was near nodded off when she arrived. She came in through the front door looking dragged down, and I kind of sat up, and then we were both just there in an odd silence.

"So?" I said.

"So," she agreed.

"What do we do?"

"Well," said Peggy, "there's the short term and

Brian Allen Carr

long term. Rent's paid, and your uncle and I share an account, so when the checks come I can put them in the bank. I don't know who all will miss him and when. I mean, he doesn't have a boss, and it's not like he had any jobs lined up. He doesn't owe anyone money. His friends might realize he's missing, but most likely his friends are the ones who left him where he was, so them snooping around makes little to no sense. You turn eighteen in a few months. At that point the checks start coming to you. I think we can keep everything about your uncle quiet until then. But it leaves us the short term." She rubbed the bridge of her nose, sat silent as if waiting.

"Okay," I said. "What about the short term."

"I need to see where he is."

That night, beneath a slight moon, Peggy and I drove to Schort Way.

"If it was a movie we'd burn it down." I imagined the house ablaze in the night. Orange fire shifting the entirety of it to wood smoke.

"That's stupid. That place catches on fire they'll know for sure. They'll come put out the fire and his dead body will be in there, and then who knows what happens to you and who knows what happens to the checks."

"Then what's the plan?"

"We gotta move him."

"Move him where?"

"You ever been to your grandfather's old place? It's northwest of here about half an hour. It's farmland, but there's a clump of forest toward the back of it, and there's an old outhouse that we could put him in, to keep him safe from coyotes, and I don't think anyone would find him for a long time. I went out there looking for him. I checked in the damn outhouse. I figured he might be there holed up and wasted. He took me there a few times. Told me about growing up. There's no houses. No people really live out that way or anything."

"When?"

"Day before yesterday. I drove up."

"I mean, when should we move him?"

Peggy took a deep breath and exhaled a plume of steam. It drifted toward the moon. "Now."

I looked at her. "And then what? You and I just live in the apartment. Pretend like it never happened?"

"When you're eighteen we can discuss it again."

"But then what's that make us? You and me?"

"It makes me your aunt, Riggle."

"Okay," I said. "Seems like a good enough plan."

I pulled my uncle from his death spot and dragged him through the snow toward his own car and his legs left a trail in the fresh powder like a slug across carpet. I heaved him into the backseat. His neck was frozen. His head didn't wibble wobble. His arms stayed stuck to his sides. I got him halfway in, circled the car, opened the other door and lugged him the rest of the way in by his shoulders. He hit the warm inside air and immediately started reeking of piss. We drove silently in the night down empty farm roads that glowed in the gleam of our headlights, and on either side of us there seemed to be a universe of nothing. Peggy and I sat quietly, I guess both of us just replaying memories of my uncle in our heads.

"How'd y'all meet?" I asked.

"Me and Joe? At a bar. I was there with some girl-friends and there was boxing on a TV, and we were play fighting with each other and Joe came up and said, 'I bet you ain't ever hit anything.' But I told him I'd been in loads of fights.

"'Let's see then,' he told me.

"'See what?'

"'What you got.'

"'You want me to hit you?'

"'I want you to try.'"

"You hit him?" I said. "That's how y'all met?"

"Nah, I didn't hit him," Peggy said. "I knocked his ass out. Two hits."

"You hitting him, him hitting the floor?"

"Nope. I hit him twice and he fell over. He came to a few minutes later, bought me a drink, and then he took me home."

Peggy only watched as I pushed my uncle from the car and lugged him across a snow-heavy field into a wooded area, and propped him inside an antique outhouse that was ramshackle and teetering. It smelled like mushrooms and old leaves, and I perched him on a board with a poop hole cut into it, and the hole disappeared into darkness.

I came out of the outhouse spent and panting, and I looked at Peggy. "Why couldn't you help?"

Peggy stood still, flakes of snow caught in her hair. "I can't touch him like that."

We propped a stone in front of the outhouse door to make sure nothing would open it, and we stepped back and considered the tiny wooden structure he rested in, not much larger than a coffin would be, and Peggy's shoulders shook, and she brought her hands to her face, and my whole body felt hot.

"I ain't thought about it yet," she said. Her voice sounded bubbly. Like how it does when your throat hurts because you're about to cry. But she lowered her hands and tears weren't streaming from her eyes like I figured.

"I mean, I knew he'd always end this way. He was sweet but he was a fuck-up. I think he got that from his dad. I never met your grandfather. But I heard stories. Your uncle thought he made the clouds."

"Yeah, I heard that one too."

Peggy's eyes found my eyes. "What was that with your hand?"

"Remote," I said. "My mom taught it to me. It was stories."

"Stories?"

"How things happened I guess. I don't know. It's lame."

"Tell me some of them someday?"

"Yeah, someday."

Peggy and I stood there in the silence for a long time. The moon seemed like a muted jewel above us.

There were no shadows. There were no sounds except our feet in the snow. I don't know how long we stayed there in that winter night, but when the day started to gray with morning, Peggy led me to the car and we drove away.

"That will work, right?" I asked.

"What?"

"Where we put him."

The dead cornfields streaked by, covered in patches of graying snow.

"Of course it will," said Peggy. "I can always figure things out."

Other Days

On March 14, we walked out of school and stood for seventeen minutes in the cold to sort of pay tribute to the kids who died in the Florida shooting. At least, some kids did. I mean, lots of them walked outside, but not everyone knew entirely why.

I think I did it the right way. I don't know exactly how I feel about guns. I don't think they should all be illegal, but I think when people die it's good to pay respect to them, and that can look a bunch of different ways. We didn't know those kids, but we knew they were kids, and so during second period, a bunch of us stood up and walked quietly down the halls.

It's amazing to me how many different types of people we have in the school, but how in so many ways we're all the same. It's hard to really explain that with words, but I know when I was standing outside, I was standing outside with people I wouldn't have done much with.

Like, if most of those kids had invited me to go to their houses and play video games, I would've said no. But I was protesting or observing or memorializing with them, and maybe that's the way it works. If you go to war, I guess you're fighting alongside a ton of people you'd rather not be with. If you get a job, even, it might be with people you'd otherwise not be around.

I mean, I still have the job at Broth, even as I write this, and I haven't hung out with anyone from work unless you want to count the conspiracy-theory waiter. And really, by hang out I mean he's given me a few rides home.

He's even asked me about my uncle. "You still haven't seen him?"

"No. Haven't talked to him or anything," I said. "Maybe Peggy has, though."

"I got a theory . . ." said the waiter.

"I bet you do," I told him. It had to do with aliens.

Chef and I talk a bunch at work, and maybe I'd hang out with her, but she wouldn't want to hang out with me. But she teaches me about food, and she gives me books to read.

A few days ago, she asked if I wanted to train to do garde-manger, which is a fancy word for salad bitch, but I was like, "I want to be a dishwasher a little while longer."

"Why?"

I was in my soggy apron and there were stacks of greasy dishes to run through, and my back was aching from being hunched over at the sinks, like I'd gotten an injection of poison right above my ass. "I'm good at it," I told her. "It feels good to be good at something."

"It feels good to be good at something, Chef," Chef said.

With Peggy—if it weren't for my uncle, she wouldn't be my aunt. She wouldn't be my friend. She wouldn't know me. But the other day, when I got home from work, she said, "You're looking older."

"Thanks," I said. I was kind of picking at my hands, because washing dishes just makes them fall apart, and there's always like bits of skin flaking off my fingers.

"Lemme see," she said to me, and she looked at my hand. "Come sit on the couch."

Her purse was with her, and she had some lotion in it that she took out, and she took my hand, and put a squirt of lotion into one of my palms, and then she sort of rubbed it in, and it was two things.

1. It was one of the kindest and most generous things she'd ever done for me.
2. It was hawt as hell, man. It was like she was giving all my fingers handjobs.

——

During the walkout when I was standing outside with my classmates, Bennet came up to me and put his hand on my shoulder. "We can memorialize him too, if you want?"

"Sure," I said, but that's the only other time my uncle has come up between us.

Then Bennet said, "Give me your phone," and he took a picture of us standing in front of the walkout crowd and tweeted it with the caption: *Strugglers*.

Maybe he was being ironic?

I still haven't heard from Erika. I text her from time to time, but I get nothing back, and who knows? Maybe she's seen it and doesn't want to respond, or maybe she doesn't have a phone anymore, or maybe she moved back to Michigan and got to hang out with her old friend Hannah again. The one she'd met in Michigan when she was younger. The white one who was nice to her the way Erika was nice to me.

Who's to say?

There are a few more things I have to tell you about.

There was another philosopher in my book named Plato, and he had this metaphor about shadows. Basically he said that we were all just watching shadows on walls. That all of life wasn't really happening. That it was just, like, pretending to happen. It's like life's a movie. And the job of all the people in the audience watching the screen is to realize that they're watching a screen. And they have to climb their way out of the theater and stumble with shocked eyes into the real light of existence. And after that they need to go back and rescue everyone else left inside.

But maybe it's best to let sleeping people sleep.

Right now I'm about to go to bed, but before I do, I want Remote to tell you how Sunday got its name, because I think it was the last story my mom ever told me:

In the time before the shadows, I realized that my only true accomplishment in life was naming the days, and I only had one day left to name so I became sad. I would spend long hours brooding, knowing that once the final task was complete, I would feel empty.

My friends noticed my sadness, and they sent me to Wed to see if he could catch my sickness and set it free in his tree. But once I was in front of him, Wed said my sadness could not be removed without destroying what Remote was. "What you need is a purpose," he told me.

"I had one once," I said. "To name the days."

"Find a new purpose," Wed said. "You can have more than one."

Remote then looked at Wed's arrow. How it aimed at the sun.

"What about that?" I asked Wed.

"About what?"

"The sun," I said. "We still know almost nothing about it."

"That's not true," Wed said. "We always know where it will be."

Then I realized what I had to do. I climbed the highest mountain on Earth, and I called out to Mun, and I told him I needed a favor.

The next day, I got all of my friends together.

Tues was there and Jupiter and Frida and Satur and we stood in front of Wed, whose sunburned penis looked miserable and ashy.

"This is my plan," I told them. And I explained how Mun would use his infinite beard to hoist me into space and to send me to the sun so that I could study it and find out what it was.

"But even if you make it," said Tues, "how will we know what you come to find out? How will you ever return?"

"I will find a way," I told them. "I will send a signal."

Weeks later, Wed stood naked holding his arrow. And he felt a weird sensation. He couldn't say exactly what, but something had changed. He scanned the world with his eyes, to see if he could catch what had shifted.

Then he realized, something was watching him from the ground. It was shaped just like Wed, and it seemed to grow from out of his feet, and it stretched across the Earth away from the sun.

He waved at it, and it waved back. He danced, and it did too. He lifted his free hand into the sky. And he held his hand a way he'd never held it before, and when he did, Remote appeared on the ground in front of him, because I was sending him my message.

"He made it!" Wed hollered. "He made it all the way!"

That is how Sunday got its name.

And Wed stood there in the sunshine. And he felt it shining on.

Of course, it can be hard to zonk out.

I see the Bicycling Confederate sometimes riding around town. Every now and then I'll hold up Remote at him, and he'll holler "honk, honk" at me like I'm making a goose.

Autistic Ross stops me when I see him. The first time he did, I held up Remote at him, and he said, "That's the farmer."

"Farmer?"

"Have you ever played Rock, Paper, Scissors?"

"Sure."

"I think it should be different," he said. "I think it should be Farmer, Garlic, Vampire."

Winter was fading, and the streets were slick with snowmelt. "I don't understand."

"Farmer beats garlic," he told me, holding up his hand like Remote. "Garlic beats vampire," he said, holding up his hand like a rock. "But vampire beats farmer." He held his hand like scissors except his fingers pointed toward the ground.

FARMER GARLIC VAMPIRE

Then we played a few games. Right there on the streets of Opioid, Indiana, for all the passersby to see.

You can play it too. But be warned it's addicting. You play it once, you'll play it forever. Teach it to others. They'll appreciate it and get addicted too. I only ask that when you do, be sure to tell everyone you learned it in Opioid, Indiana.

For book club discussion questions on
Brian Allen Carr's *Opioid, Indiana*,
please visit bit.ly/opioidindianadiscussionquestions